Trial
By Fire

AVALON

WEB OF MAGIC

Book 6

TRIAL BY FIRE

RACHEL ROBERTS

Seven Seas

TRIAL BY FIRE

Published by Seven Seas Entertainment.

ISBN: 978-1-934876-49-7

Cover and interior illustrations by Allison Strom

Interior book design by
Pauline Neuwirth, Neuwirth & Associates, Inc.

10 9 8 7 6 5 4 3 2 1

Printed in Canada

1

D ARK CLOUDS SLID over twin moons, covering the night like a blanket. Behind the swirling mist, stars fell like tears as earth, mountain, and sky faded away.

A lone howl pierced the blackness.

Once tens of thousands strong, the pack now numbered little over a hundred. Since the erosion of magic from Aldenmor, the mistwolves had been hunted, feared as enemies, and slaughtered by creatures that had risen in the shadows of darkness. With his ears pressed back, Moonshadow felt what his ancestors had once felt. He knew what they had known. The mistwolves were strong, proud protectors. Then, as now, they were the guardians of Aldenmor.

Above, colors rippled across the heavens as if strewn by some painter's wild brush. Fiery red, ocean blue, brilliant yellow, and deep forest green curled and danced, a pulsating patchwork that flowed across the sky.

Faint howls, a chorus of spirits, echoed from the past, rising into one song, the collective song of ages: the wolfsong.

The night trembled as mistwolves, hundreds, then thousands strong, thundered down the spirit trail.

"Run with us!"

Swept into the song of the mistwolves, the power of the mystical vision grew and Moonshadow ran. Towering canyons, fertile plains, immense forests full of life swept past as the spirit pack came upon the land's edge, where sand and sea met, where worlds joined. Thousands of mistwolves stood upon the beachhead, ghostly forms glistening before the crystal city. Sparkling towers rose, catching glints of sun and spray. Creatures of untold power and magic inhabited the city, sharing its wonders with the world of humans. Families of griffins and dragons circled the skies. Unicorns big and small ran free through the resplendent gardens playing with human students of magic. Sea dragons and merfolk crested the tides, waving and smiling as the pack stood at the edge of forever.

"My spirit sings to be with you!" the lone mistwolf cried out.

"Take from the past and lead us into the future, Moonshadow."

Lightning flashed—the broken city lay in pieces. And in the half-light, every tower was covered in webs. Spiders climbed over the ruins, weaving darkness onto the magic web itself. He could hear the pack singing, mournful weeping howls, as they faded like tracks in the dust. Now holding only memories, the home of magic closed like a tomb.

Moonshadow, leader of the mistwolves, sat alone on the peak of Mount Hope. Tilting his head toward Aldenmor's rising sun, the mighty pack leader tried to draw as much strength from his ancestors as he could. But the vision had ended.

At last, the mistwolf opened his golden eyes. Moonshadow's heart ached. The once glorious realm of Aldenmor lay before him in ruins—ravaged by Black Fire, devoid of trees and grass, burnt and scarred by the dark magic.

Moonshadow howled into the wind, crying for what was lost. His cry lingered, echoing across the Shadowlands. Then all was silent.

For a moment, sweet smells of fresh grass, cool springs, and new life filled the air. Moonshadow knew then what his spirit vision meant. Even in the darkest hour, the spirit pack's images spoke of hope, of humans and magical creatures working together as in ancient times. Moonshadow held the promise of hope to his chest as he shook morning dew from his coat. He felt the cool object dangling around his neck. The fairy map, a magical talisman given to him by the Fairimentals and Adriane, his human wolf sister. He'd been using the fairy map to guide the pack through the portals on Aldenmor in an attempt to defend the land from the Dark Sorceress. She was rapidly destroying the planet, stealing magic from the animals and storing it in giant crystals. Storing magic in the crystal constructions was dangerous—her earlier attempts had failed, causing massive Black Fire fallout. But now she had three stable crystals—waiting for an influx of magic.

Even with the help of the fairy map, the battle to protect Aldenmor was being slowly lost. Time and magic were running out.

The facets of the talisman flashed and twinkled in the rays of the morning sun. Moonshadow thought again of his vision and suddenly wondered if the map had been given to him for a different purpose altogether. Yes, he was sure of it. This fairy map, given to him to protect, was a key to the salvation of Aldenmor—and of Avalon.

If only he could contact the Fairimentals. They would know what he was supposed to do, but the Fairy Glen had been cut off. No one had been able to reach it or the Fairimentals for weeks.

Suddenly, the fur on the back of Moonshadow's neck stood up. He sniffed at the air. Something smelled foul. Perhaps wafts of further decay from the Shadowlands—

the howl cut through his thoughts as a giant gray mist-wolf broke through the brush.

"Come quickly," the wolf called. *"The mistwolves are under attack!"*

Moonshadow leaped to his feet and turned toward his approaching wolf brother. *"Who dares to attack the mist-wolves?"* the pack leader asked.

"I do," the mistwolf replied, fiercely baring long, sharp teeth.

Moonshadow tensed. But before he could move, searing pain lanced into his shoulder. He fell to his knees as another lash tore across his back, pain washing over him in waves of agony. Snarling and short of breath, he saw the riders appear, as if out of thin air. Thick bodies sat heavily on their mounts, eyes gleaming menacing green through the ports of steel helmets. Sharp, serrated teeth grinned wildly from stout heads with pointed ears. They wore leather armor and spiked boots, and held long whips that dripped green venom. Goblins. And they were riding night stallions. The fiendish giant mounts snorted bursts of fire as their eyes glowed demon red. Jet-black imps dangled a glowing net between them.

Ropes could not hold a mistwolf—even this traitor should know that. Moonshadow concentrated on releasing his spirit from his physical body. He closed his eyes and summoned his magic, waiting for the feeling of lightness that came when he turned to mist. But he couldn't. He was locked in place, as if something was controlling his magic.

The net flew over the mighty wolf. He felt fire digging into his sides, tightening around his neck. He desperately tried to turn to mist, but every struggle increased the net's hold over him.

"White Fang! Dawnrunner!" Moonshadow howled in fury for his packmates.

"Don't bother," the gray wolf snarled at the pack leader. *"We already have the others. You are the last."*

The riders shouted in oblique, rough tongues as their night stallions snorted, encircling the wolf. The pack leader made no further move to escape, knowing it would only suffocate him. Instead, he slowed his panting and moved his mind away from the pain. Growling low, he struggled to see past the night stallions' long legs. He needed to identify the traitor.

Moonshadow locked eyes with the wolf that had dared to betray the pack. The net was yanked tight as the goblin riders pulled the wolf leader down hard. But Moonshadow no longer felt the pain. He kept his eyes on the traitor wolf.

The goblin riders jeered before kicking their mounts, dragging Moonshadow behind them.

Alone on the peak, the traitor watched the riders disappear into the valley of dark shadows below. Golden eyes flickered fiery red as smooth fur shimmered, dissolving into scales. The wolf's body flowed and twisted as it

rose up on its two hind legs. A lizard-shaped head twisted free with a mouthful of pointed teeth. Long scaly legs with splayed feet stood tall, and webbed nails sharpened into claws as the Skultum assumed his true form.

2

*K*ARA DAVIES WATCHED the fire dance behind the ornate wrought-iron screen. The fireplace tools stood to the right in a metal basket tipped with animal claws. The sides of the hearth were trimmed with stone wings. Just about everything in Ravenswood Manor had been inspired or influenced by animals. Some were easily recognizable, like the famous wildlife paintings of lions hunting the Serengeti, Siberian tigers from India, massive grizzlies from the Canadian northwest, wild horses running across the open Dakota plains. Other objects hinted at more unusual creatures: a unicorn engraving in the wood paneling, a dragonhead of ebony set on chair arms. If you didn't know better, these were merely decorative touches inspired by fanciful myths and legends.

But Kara Davies, Emily Fletcher, and Adriane Charday knew that fantastic creatures like these still existed. At one time, these amazing creatures were plentiful. But like so many great species of Earth caught forever frozen in paintings and pieces of ornamental art, there were very few, if any, real ones left.

Perhaps that was why the guardians of the magical world of Aldenmor, known as Fairimentals, had sent for the girls, enfolding them in a mystery as profound as the magic itself. Three among millions had been chosen, gifted with the magic. Their lives were now bound forever with animals and creatures they used to think only lived in fairy tales.

Shadows coiled across the rows of stacked books as Kara took in warmth and comfort from the Ravenswood Manor library. She gazed out the windows overlooking the great lawn behind the manor house. Many creatures had come to Ravenswood for refuge. The animals out there weren't paintings, they were real. So many endangered and lost. How could she, Emily, and Adriane protect them when they were just learning about the magic themselves? How could she help them when she couldn't even help herself?

Lyra, the big orange spotted cat, arched her back and stretched long front legs. *"You're thinking again,"* she purred.

"I do have a brain, you know," the blond-haired girl quipped. "Contrary to popular opinion."

"I didn't say anything."

Kara regarded the furry ferret sitting at the computer station on one of the shelves of the library wall. When the girls were not using the library as their headquarters, the computer remained hidden behind a sliding bookcase.

Ozzie, the fuzzy former elf, had become quite a pro on the computer. He loved dealing with all the email from the fans of Ravenswood. Ozzie had also found a very useful place for himself reviewing and cataloging the mass of information Mr. Gardener, the owner of Ravenswood, had left behind before vanishing.

The list of animals scrolling down the screen had grown since the girls had first met the magical ferret back at the end of August. Some fifty creatures, big and small, now resided here along with deer, peacocks, and birds. There were a lot of animals to watch over. Winter was coming. Normally at this time of year, Kara was all about Thanksgiving with friends and family, Christmas trees, parties and presents, ice-skating, and hot chocolate. Now all she thought about was how they were going to feed so many hungry and cold creatures. Depressing thoughts. This was her responsibility. She had convinced her father, the mayor of Stonehill, to let the girls take care of Ravenswood. So many were counting on her, and so far, she had failed miserably.

Though the room was toasty warm, Kara shivered at the memory of what had happened at the Ravenswood Benefit Concert last weekend. She had dabbled in a form of magic called spellsinging, and it had backfired big time. The Dark Sorceress had sent an evil shape-shifting Skultum who tricked Kara into opening the fairy map to Avalon, the mysterious goal of their quest.

Her friends saved her. By spellsinging together, Emily and Adriane had broken the spell over Kara and helped her banish the shape-shifter. But not before the fairy map had revealed a pathway of portals. For all she knew, she had handed their enemy an open door to the home of all magic.

Since then, Kara had fallen into despair, questioning her ability to do anything right and her role as the blazing star. And underneath it all was the fear that she was changing, careening away from her life as it had been before magic, plunging headlong into some weird other place.

"I just finished unloading three truckloads of supplies!" Adriane's voice cut through Kara's thoughts as the tall, dark-haired girl bounded into the library followed by Stormbringer, the mistwolf. "Where were you?"

"I was doing some homework." Kara casually gestured to her pile of closed schoolbooks neatly stacked on the oak reading table.

Adriane opened her mouth to comment, but Storm stopped her with a gentle nudge. The warrior shrugged and flopped onto one of the large velvet pillows on the sofa, pulling Storm into a big hug. The great silver mist-wolf sprawled over the girl.

"That was a good run." Though she didn't speak out loud, Adriane heard Storm clearly in her head. Lyra could communicate in the same way.

"Gran's had us running all over the place," Adriane said. "Salt strips had to be set up for the deer, and I had to prepare food blends to include turkey, pheasants, quail . . . and quiffles."

Kara wasn't listening. She just stared into the crackling fire.

Adriane frowned. She had never seen Kara like this before. And she didn't like it.

They had come a long way together in a few months. When she'd first met Kara, she thought her shallow as a rain puddle. Now she knew that underneath that perfectly coordinated exterior was a real brain, a real heart, and some incredible magical power. Kara was truly a blazing star.

Emily was a natural healer. In the beginning she helped Kara and Adriane see eye-to-eye, which hadn't been easy. Kara certainly wasn't afraid to express her opinions and Adriane's warrior temper wasn't easy to keep in check. But in the end, what mattered was that they had taken care of one another and, against all odds, forged a bond of friendship.

Everyone was concerned about Kara's unusual depression, aware of how deeply the Skultum's spell had affected her. Even her friends at school had noticed

Kara's obvious retreat from the normal boisterous, self-assured, perfect being of total cool.

Suddenly, the door burst open. "Mail call!" Emily Fletcher announced as she hurried inside. "Get yer latest copy of the Stonehill Gazette."

A small herd of creatures followed the bundled red-headed girl, including Ronif, Balthazar, Rommel, and Rasha, trusted magical friends. While the pegasi, quiffles, and wommels warmed themselves in front of the fire, Emily dropped her backpack to rub her hands together. Her cheeks were pink with cold. "How's it going, Ozzie?" She looked over the ferret's head as he pounded away on the keys.

"I put all the new emails in your 'to be answered' file."

"Take a break. Look what I brought." Emily pulled four boxes of graham crackers, a dozen chocolate bars, and a bag of marshmallows out of her backpack, dangling the goodies in front of Ozzie's face.

The ferret's eyes practically bugged out of his furry head. "OooO! What's that?"

"Come on, I'll show you," Emily giggled, walking over to the fireplace.

Ozzie followed her and the tantalizing bag of white marshmallows.

Kara was still staring out the window.

Emily glanced from Kara to Adriane as she pulled out a bunch of long wooden sticks from her pack, handing them to each of the animals.

"The feed supplies arrived," Adriane said, taking a stick and nestling herself between Rommel and Rasha. She deftly stuck a marshmallow onto the end of the stick as the others watched, fascinated.

"Lemme see that." Ozzie stuck his nose in the bag of mallows and speared four onto his stick at once.

"Storm and I spotted whitetail, black, and mule deer," Adriane continued. "With winter closing in, the food plots have to be set out constantly now along with salt strips. The animals are going to get very hungry."

Ozzie stuffed two marshmallows into his mouth. "Yum!"

"Wait, Ozzie," Emily instructed. "You have to toast the marshmallow and make a sandwich on the crackers."

Adriane, Emily, Ozzie, and the others gathered around the fireplace armed with wooden sticks. "With the new landmark status, the town council has allocated funds for food, but a lot of our animals are just not eating," Adriane said to Ronif the quiffle.

"*They are restless and homesick,*" Storm said.

"And not everyone is used to cold weather," Rasha added. "Most come from warmer climates."

Emily ruffled Rasha's head feathers. "Hopefully, you'll all be back home soon."

"Right back in the sorceress's dungeon," Kara grumbled.

Adriane's eyes flashed. "That's positive thinking, Barbie."

Kara turned away, golden hair covering her face. "I believed in Johnny and got burned big time."

Emily sighed. "That wasn't your fault."

"Dark fairy magic is very strong, especially from a trickster like the Skultum," Rasha said.

"We were all fooled," Adriane reminded her. "The thing had me under its spell, too."

"Well, what do you think we should do?" Kara asked, suddenly aware of how much she hated feeling helpless and scared. "We can't control our powers, we haven't heard from the Fairimentals in weeks, and the Dark Sorceress could be in Avalon as we speak."

"We don't know that, Kara," Emily said. "We stopped the Skultum and took the map back."

The girls glanced at the glowing orb sitting on the reading table. Inside a pattern of stars twinkled.

"We can't just keep sitting around waiting," Adriane stated. "What if the sorceress attacks Ravenswood?"

"DAhh!" Ozzie pulled a flaming stick out of the fire, waving it around his head.

"Careful, Ozzie!" Adriane exclaimed, covering her hair.

Ronif and Rasha weren't faring much better, each losing their marshmallows to the hungry flames.

"You're doing it wrong," Kara said softly.

"What?"

"Here. Give me that." Kara took the wooden stick from Ozzie's paw and speared a marshmallow. "You have to lightly brown the marshmallow without letting it burn. See?"

Kara held it over the flame, slowly twirling it until it was golden brown.

"Ooo. That's very good."

The animals all nodded in agreement.

"Then," Kara continued, "you place it between *two* layers of chocolate. This way the chocolate covers both graham crackers."

"She's a genius!" Ronif exclaimed.

Emily and Adriane suppressed smiles.

The others, except for Storm and Lyra, followed suit. Soon Ozzie was happily covered in melted marshmallow fluff, chocolate, and crumbs.

Adriane picked up the paper Emily had brought in. The front page displayed a picture of Mrs. Beasley Windor and the town council. Windor was holding a landmark status certificate for Ravenswood. The headline read: RAVENSWOOD A ROARING SUCCESS. PUTS STONEHILL ON THE MAP.

Adriane snorted. "Look at this. Windor hated the idea of Ravenswood from the start, and now she is totally taking credit for our success!"

"That's politics," Emily said. "All things considered, we should be grateful. Why do you think we were able to get the funds for the winter supplies so fast? Windor personally approved the invoices!"

"Yeah, but I still don't have to like it." Adriane threw the paper down.

"Even with the supplies, what if we get more refugees from Aldenmor?" Balthazar, the pegasus, asked. "We can't turn them away."

Ronif waddled over, testing a marshmallow sandwich in his rubbery beak. "Even with the tours closed for the cold season, someone is bound to discover us."

Ronif was right. Even on a preserve as big as Ravenswood, the mages could not hide all of the refugees forever. Although it seemed Mrs. Windor was on their side now, they all knew how quickly things could change.

Kara picked up the newspaper and regarded the picture. Yes, the girls had pulled off the concert and fooled the whole crowd into thinking that the magical battle they saw was all part of the show. But still, the evil shape-shifting Skultum pretending to be pop star Johnny Conrad had put Kara under its spell. It had tapped into her blazing star magic, and to Kara's horror she had discovered the magic to be dark and ugly. That was no illusion.

"Kawaaa," Ozzie jumped onto the table, his mouth exploding with marshmallows. "Makemee sommmorre!"

"The Fairimentals should have made you a pig instead of a ferret," Kara commented.

Pop! The fire surged upward in the hearth with a huge crackle, startling the group.

"How are you doing with the email search for Be*Tween?" Emily asked Ozzie.

"Nothing new," Ozzie remarked. "I've tried replying a dozen times but wherever that email came from, it can't be traced."

Ozzie was referring to a message sent from the magical musical group known as Be*Tween. From somewhere on the magic web, they had told the girls to stand strong and be ready. Their time was coming.

The ferret munched thoughtfully on another s'more. "Be*Tween didn't give us much information."

"Maybe they couldn't," Rasha said around a mouth full of mallows. "Afraid they might get caught."

"Hey, watch the fur," Storm rumbled, licking a dollop of melted marshmallow off her shimmering coat.

"Sorry," Ozzie said, holding the stick of marshmallows behind him as he faced the group.

Sparks leaped from the crackling logs, licking at the six melting marshmallows the ferret had crammed onto his stick.

"Be careful, Ozzie," Ronif complained. "That's hot!"

"And it smells awful." The ferret scrunched his marshmallow mustache, sniffing the air around him. "Smells like—"

"Ozzie!" Emily yelled.

"Your tail's on fire," Balthazar observed.

"Huh?" Ozzie looked over his shoulder. *"Ahhhh!"*

The ferret tossed his marshmallows as he ran across the room, a plume of smoke trailing him. Everyone jumped out of the way, grabbing rugs, towels, and anything they could find to throw over the smoking ferret.

Kara grabbed a vase from an end table, pulled out the flowers, and emptied the water over Ozzie.

"BluB!"

Smoke hissed from the soaked ferret.

"Are you okay, Ozzie?" Emily asked, hoisting him upside down to examine his tail.

"Watch it! Watch it!"

"Hold still." Emily's rainbow jewel pulsed with blue healing light. It bathed the ferret in a cool glow. "How's that?"

"Put me down!"

The soft lights in the library flickered and went dark.

The girls looked around. Smoke was slowly encircling the room.

"We blow a fuse?" Adriane asked.

The fireplace blazed, flames leaping high, sending sparks into the air as shadows skittered across the walls.

Suddenly, the fire hissed and with a loud *Pop!* flames leaped out, licking at the mantel.

The s'more eaters scrambled back.

"The fire's too big!" Adriane yelled.

With a shudder, flames erupted from the stone hearth, pushing aside the screen to roll across the rug in a fiery wave.

Hsssssssssssss.

Like snakes, tendrils of flame reached up and coiled around themselves.

"Get the extinguisher!" Emily yelled.

"Wait," Lyra told the girls. The big cat was on her feet, fur standing along the scruff of her neck.

"It's not burning anything." Ronif pointed a wing at the rug.

The fire was now completely outside the fireplace, on the carpet in the center of the room. The flames left no mark on what they touched, as if the fire were merely a ghost.

Swirling yellow, red, and blue flames reached to the domed ceiling of the library.

They formed a figure, shimmering and glowing before the group.

"A Fairimental!" Eddie the brimbee exclaimed.

"It's a *Fire*mental!" Balthazar said, astonished. "The most powerful and dangerous of the Fairimentals."

"We thought you were lost!" Ozzie's fur stood out as he leaped to his feet.

The fiery figure reached with flaming arms toward Kara.

The blond girl squealed and stepped back.

"Stand still, Kara!" Adriane urged.

Kara stood motionless as a writhing river of fire swept up the fairy map. A tendril snapped like a whip and the portals expanded, wrapping Kara in a blazing web of fire.

"You opened the portalsss!" the Firemental hissed at her.

Kara winced. It was not the fire that burned her, but the heat of her own shame.

"I . . . I'm sorry . . . I don't know what I did. I messed up really bad. And now the Dark Sorceress is all over Avalon . . ."

"The witch waitsssss in her lair."

Kara's eyes widened. "The sorceress is not in Avalon?"

"She needssss map."

Kara looked at the pattern of portals burning along the fairy map. "We'll never let her get it again!"

"There isss another . . ."

"Another map?" Kara felt desperate waves of magic as the Firemental struggled to hold itself together. She barely heard the small voice hissing in her ear.

"Follow your path, blazing ssstar, and ssssave Aldenmor."

The Firemental whirled around the room, encircling the three mages.

With a final spatter, it flickered out.

"Wait!" Adriane gasped. "Come back."

The fairy map cooled to a small silver-blue orb and came to rest in Kara's hand.

"Is everyone all right?" Emily scanned the room, making sure no one was burned.

"I've never seen anything like that before!" Balthazar exclaimed.

Lyra stood next to Kara, flicking her tail. *"If they risked sending a Firemental, things must be bad on Aldenmor."*

"There's a second fairy map!" Ozzie exclaimed.

"The only other map I know of . . . ," Adriane began slowly, "belongs to Moonshadow."

Emily looked worried. "If the Dark Sorceress needs the other map—"

"She's going to go after the mistwolves," Adriane finished.

"We must warn them." Storm paced.

"Why would she need another map if she already knows what's in this one?" Ronif asked.

"Maybe she doesn't," Kara said hopefully.

"Maybe she needs a second map to open other portals," Rasha suggested.

The warrior got to her feet. "Either way, there's still time. We have to get to Moonshadow before the Dark Sorceress and we have to get to Avalon first." Adriane pounded her fist. "It's the only way to save Aldenmor. I know it!" A quick glance at her friends told Adriane that they were all thinking the same thing. Without Avalon's magic, Aldenmor would be lost.

"Remember when the Fairimentals first came to us at the glade?" Adriane asked.

Emily nodded. "They told us to find Avalon."

"And that's what Kara was doing."

Kara's eyes flew open wide. "So maybe . . . I did good."

"You do have a knack for using magic in unusually lucky ways," Adriane smiled wryly.

"Kara." Emily stepped in front of the blond girl. "Whatever you did, we know you *meant* to do good and that's what counts."

"That's right!" Ozzie leaned over the table to hug Kara. "We're always with you no matter what!"

The animals converged on Kara in warm hugs.

Kara flushed but smiled, holding the gooey ferret away from her sweater.

"Thanks." She placed Ozzie back on the rug.

The Firemental had said to follow her path. She had worried that her blazing star magic would send her spiraling out of control, burning out in a blaze of glory. She felt the fire roiling at the very core of her being. Well, whatever blazed inside her, it was time to let it free!

Kara tossed her golden hair over a shoulder, forging ahead before she could stop to think about what she was saying. "If we're going to save Aldenmor, we've got to stop talking about it and *do* it!"

The room was silent. They all knew Kara was right. The time had come for the girls to put all they had learned to the test. To act now. Or it would be too late.

"We'll use the unicorn horn and open the portal here on Ravenswood," Kara said. "Just like I did before."

"It's time." Emily took Kara's and Adriane's hands in hers.

Lyra pushed her large head into Kara's side. *"Time to stand together."*

"Time to save our friends!" Storm stood between the mages.

"The Fairimentals chose me to choose you." Ozzie stood tall, puffing out his furry chest. "Now let's all choose to do what we were chosen for. Let's go!"

Ronif and Rasha looked at one another as the sticky ferret whizzed by and charged out of the library.

"We'll bring the unicorn horn and the fairy map," Kara said, racing ahead before she could change her mind. "The magic of the horn should keep us safe."

"I'll tell Gran we're going on a school trip," Adriane said.

"I'll get the Pet Palace shut down," Emily said.

"I'll go pack," Kara concluded firmly.

Everyone looked at Kara.

"What?" she shrugged. "I'm not going without a change of clothes!"

"Good to have you back, Kara," Emily smiled.

Kara grinned and glanced at Adriane.

The dark-haired girl raised her fist and touched Kara's fist. "Okay, we'll meet at the portal field in half an hour."

"What should we tell the others?" asked Ronif.

"Tell them to get ready!" Kara said. "We're going to bring them home."

3

*T*HE NOON SUN broke through patchwork clouds as animals filled the large field in the northwest quadrant of the wildlife preserve. It was here they had first appeared in Ravenswood—wommels, brimbees, pegasi, jeeran, and all the others, desperately rushing through the hidden doorway from their world to be healed.

The surrounding forest was already thinning as maples and oaks offered their final gift of colors. Soon they would submit to their cold slumber. Only the never-changing greens of the pines would tough it out until spring.

Emily, Adriane, Kara, Lyra, Storm, and Ozzie made their way through the throng of adoring, cheering creatures. Rasha, Ronif, and Balthazar followed, setting off another round of hoots, hollers, neighs, and chirps. Word had spread fast that the girls had been called by the Firemental. Three young mages and their magical animal friends were going to save their world.

Ozzie spoke first.

"When I first met the Fairimentals," he began, "they told me I would play a part in fighting dark magic and saving our world. I'm a ferr—an elf! I didn't believe it possible. Now, I'm here to tell you I believe!" The ferret raised his furry arms dramatically as the crowd reacted with more cheers.

"I believe in our friends and I believe in the magic." Ozzie began shuffling back and forth, calling out to the crowd. "And with a little luck, you'll all see home again." He dropped to one knee, arms outstretched. "You just have to believe!"

More cheers met Ozzie's impassioned speech. They all needed to hear those words. Uncertainties lay ahead. The girls knew it. Their journey together had been as unpredictable as it had been rewarding. Yet each knew one thing for sure—something the Fairimentals had told them: There is no going back.

Did they really believe they could do what they were chosen for?

Emily thought about how far she'd come. Her first magical friend, a fairy creature called Phel, had taught her healing was more than knowledge of medicine and technique, it was rooted deep in compassion and empathy.

Now she would have to help heal a whole world. Had she learned enough to handle it?

Adriane looked at her amber wolfstone set in the onyx and turquoise band on her wrist. The silver mistwolf beside her matched the reflective stripes down the sides of Adriane's black track pants. Headstrong, Adriane had always fought with an iron will, barreling forward in a straight line, determined to find her own name, her own place. Thanks to Stormbringer, she knew she was not just a fighter, but a warrior with courage to soar free like a . . . bird. She smiled. No, to run free like a wolf. She was bonded forever to the mistwolves and Stormbringer.

"Packmates," Storm said, looking at her with deep golden eyes.

With Storm at her side, Adriane could do anything.

"All right, Ronif, Rasha, Balthazar, you're in charge now," Emily said. "Just try to keep everyone's spirits up."

"We will do our best," Balthazar said.

"As soon as the portal opens, call to Moonshadow and Silver Eyes," Adriane told Storm. "See if you can get a reading on what's going on over there."

"I will try." Storm remained ever calm, ever strong.

"I think I have everything," Kara said, brushing her long hair back while rummaging in her bright red backpack. Lyra stood beside her, grooming her own lustrous spotted fur. Kara was wearing designer hiking boots, dark denim jeans, and a faux fur-trimmed safari coat.

Kara was beginning to understand that her journey

was tied to the magic more than anyone had thought possible. She was the conductor. With her, magic shone in endless circles, spreading like the brilliance of her smile. It had a profound effect on everyone—human and animal—she came into contact with. But just as still waters ran deep, she felt something more, a darkness just below the surface, waiting to drag her down.

"Kara, you have the fairy map?" Emily asked.

"Fairy map, check." She lifted the glowing ball from her pack. Tiny star patterns sparkled inside, a key to the pathways of the web.

Everyone looked with awe upon the gift given to Kara by the Fairimentals. With this map, Kara had opened pathways of portals to parts unknown on the magic web.

"Unicorn horn?" Adriane asked.

"Right here," Kara held up the horn. Sunlight split the crystal sending sparkles racing up and down the swirled horn.

"Kara, what else is in there?" Emily asked, curiously eyeing her bulging backpack.

"Just some essentials," Kara replied. "Granola bars, a toothbrush, hairspray, Breath Blast, hair clips, a change of socks, some lip balm, chips . . ."

"Where do you think we're going? Paris?" Adriane asked.

"Well, we don't really know, do we?" Kara shot back.

"Let's find out," Emily said.

Kara held the unicorn horn up high.

The crowd fanned out giving the mages room.

The three girls stood close together, Ozzie before them, Lyra and Storm on either side.

Slowly, Adriane reached out and grasped Kara's hand, wrapping her fingers around it and the unicorn horn. Adriane's wolf stone glinted, then glowed bright gold.

Then Emily reached out, adding her hand to the others. Her rainbow jewel flared to life with blue-green light.

The crowd fell silent as spirals of amber and blue-green magic raced from the jewels and swirled around the girls' arms. They could feel the animals in the field adding their own individual strength, helping to focus the magic.

"Okay, here we go." Kara felt the magic surging though her. She recognized it and opened herself as it built, rising into waves of power, using her as a vehicle for its release. Pushing the fear from her mind, she focused and bent the power to her will.

"Concentrate on the dreamcatcher," Emily said, closing her eyes. "Picture it opening!"

A hidden, magical dreamcatcher protected the portal. It was constructed from strands of the magic web itself.

Power surged from Adriane's and Emily's jewels and flowed through Kara, around her body, up her arms, and right into the horn of the unicorn. A stream of magic fire burst from the crystal horn, skyrocketing in a wild blaze of colors.

"Hold it steady!" Adriane yelled.

Kara whirled the beam of crystal starlight in a giant circle, slicing the air with twinkles. The immense dreamcatcher appeared before them, hanging in the air just above the ground.

Lightning sparked even though there was no sign of a storm. The meadow below them suddenly lurched as thunder rolled and the immense portal swirled open. Winking stars that seemed to sit on glowing lines stretched into the distance behind the dreamcatcher. Although the girls had seen it before, looking onto the expanse of the magic web was breathtaking. Each star was a portal, connecting to countless worlds. It was beautiful, incredible—and dangerous.

"Next stop, Aldenmor!" Kara exclaimed.

Emily drew in a breath. "Here we go," she murmured. Ozzie scampered up her arm to perch on her shoulder

"Stay close," Adriane instructed, hand on Storm's neck. "Concentrate on forming a single protective bubble so we don't get separated."

The magic danced faster and faster around them. Gold, blue, and silver lit the field with dazzling brightness.

The center of the dreamcatcher opened wide before them.

"One jumps—" Adriane said.

"—we all jump!" Kara finished.

And with that, Emily, Adriane, Kara, Ozzie, Lyra, and Storm leaped through the dreamcatcher into the portal beyond.

"Emily!" Ozzie cried, grasping the healer's neck

"I've got you!" she shouted back.

Triggered by the immense power of the web, magic flew from Emily's rainbow jewel, Adriane's wolf stone, and the unicorn horn held by Kara. At once, an amber bubble covered in crackling blue light encircled them.

The bubble floated above the strands of stars like a giant balloon.

"It's awesome!" Kara exclaimed.

Emily quickly took count to make sure they were all still together. "It's okay,

Ozzie. You can open your eyes."

The ferret open one eye and gazed through the translucent bubble at the vast expanse.

"Gah!"

The web spread out before them like a galaxy. Pinpoints sparkled, but it was impossible to tell how far away the portals were—or how close.

"Hey, aren't we supposed to go directly to Aldenmor?" Ozzie asked.

"The portals must have changed to match the fairy map," Emily answered.

"All right, Barbie, you're up," Adriane said.

Kara raised the fairy map. The small sphere slowly rotated in her hand.

"Look!" Kara gasped as a pathway of portals lit up inside the fairy map like a constellation of stars.

Adriane's keen eyes flickered to the fairy map. She pointed to the same configuration of stars along the magic web. "Emily's right."

Suddenly Storm let out a sharp bark.

"Storm, what is it?" The warrior's attention was instantly drawn to her packmate.

"Something has happened to Moonshadow," Storm growled.

"What?" Adriane asked worriedly.

"I can't get a clear picture, but the pack needs help. They wait for us with Zach at Mount Hope."

Everyone exchanged worried glances. First the Firemental had appeared, and now this. Something was seriously wrong on Aldenmor.

"We have to get to Mount Hope," Adriane stated. "Now."

Kara nodded. "Okay, but which portal?" She waved her arm at the mass of bright points sprawled along the web.

"Somewhere over there." Storm fretted, pointing her nose toward a brilliant cluster of stars.

"How do we steer this thing?" Ozzie asked.

Kara held up the fairy map and matched the portals to where Storm had pointed. "Focus on the brightest star."

With a quick glance at the map, Adriane pointed to their right. "That way."

The mages raised their fists and sent the bubble floating toward the first portal, winking in the distance.

The bubble quickly picked up speed as it slid between golden strands.

"Take us down!" Adriane commanded.

With a wave of their arms, the bubble dropped onto a glittering highway of light.

"Stay away from the broken strands." Emily pointed to a section of web that hung broken and tangled.

"I thought the unicorns were fixing the web," Kara said.

Emily thought of her unicorn friend, Lorelei. Unicorns ran along the strands of the web itself, repairing it so magic could flow where it was supposed to go. But here huge swaths of web were horribly distorted, sparking like downed electrical cables. How could the unicorns hope to repair such immense damage?

"Heads up!" Adriane raised her fists, jumping the bubble over a wide gap of broken strands.

"What I wouldn't give for a flobbin right now," Ozzie commented, remembering the magic tracking creature who'd helped them navigate the web.

Emily pointed to the unicorn horn in Kara's hand. The crystal pulsed with diamond light. "Lorelei's horn," Emily said. "She gave us the magic of the unicorns."

The girls once again held hands as Kara raised the horn.

"Lorelei!" Emily called out. "Take us to Mount Hope!"

Instantly, the bubble took a sharp dip, spiraling into a

sweeping curve, right toward a knot of broken, tangled strands. A massive stargate flared dangerously ahead.

"Not that way!" Ozzie yelled, trying to push the bubble in the opposite direction.

"Hang on!" Adriane shouted.

"To what?"

Flash!

—dead silence—

For a split second, everyone was silhouetted in a blaze of white—then the web appeared, hurtling around them as they shot from the open portal.

Stars became streaks as the bubble careened down layers of strands, blazing onto a different path.

Adriane held onto the fur of Storm's neck as the bubble twisted, picking up more speed. Its thin walls were beginning to stretch, sizzling with power.

"Keep focused!" Kara shouted. "Hold it together!"

The bubble spun violently, dropped like a roller coaster and—

Flash!

—rocketed though another portal like a meteor.

Emily lost her grip and was thrown against the wall of the bubble. Electricity sparked from her jewel, sending magic fire racing around the orb. She reached out and snatched Ozzie's leg before he bounced away.

Kara and Lyra were flattened against the other side. Wild energy crackled along the bubble. Kara felt her hand push right through the wall!

"It's breaking up!" Kara yelled. Wind whipped around them, loud as a tornado. "We've got to stay together!"

Emily and Adriane strained forward, reaching to grasp hands, but the forces pulling them apart were too strong.

"Something's coming up fast!" Ozzie screamed, falling over Emily's head.

Ahead of them, a tight cluster of shimmering stars was getting bigger by the second.

"It's a nexus!" Emily called out.

The nexus hung like a thickly woven platform of light. Surrounding it were dozens of portals. Here, strands of the web interconnected, each portal leading to a different destination.

"Which portal?" Kara cried as the bubble careened headlong toward the nexus.

"Stay together!" Adriane commanded, reaching for her friends as Storm braced her legs.

"As long as we stay together, we'll be okay," Emily called, hand outstretched, trying to inch her way toward Adriane.

"We're coming in too fast!" Ozzie screamed.

Kara reached for her friends.

"We're going to hit!" Adriane yelled.

The bubble careened toward the nexus floor and spun out of control.

"Ahhh!"

Adriane clung to Storm. Ozzie buried his head in Emily's neck. Lyra's magical wings flared open to protect Kara.

The bubble hit hard, bouncing into the air, coming down again, skidding and rolling. In a sudden blast of twinkling lights, the protective orb ripped apart.

Everyone was thrown in different directions.

"Emily!"

"Adriane!"

"Mommy elf!"

Instantly, a blue-green bubble formed around Emily and Ozzie.

An amber bubble engulfed Adriane and Storm.

Diamond power blazed from the horn in Kara's hand, wrapping her and Lyra in a crystal cocoon.

They smashed into the nexus and vanished, swallowed into three different portals.

4

WIND WHIPPED WAVES of white, wrapping Adriane in cold. She covered her face, trying to see through the blizzard, thankful she had worn a down vest and heavy sweater.

"Storm?" she called out, suddenly afraid her friend had landed some place far from her.

"*I am here*," the wolf answered.

Adriane turned at the sound of the voice in her head. She instantly felt better.

She pulled her wool hat tight over her ears and trudged, head low, through the heavy snow. Within seconds, she found Storm. Dropping to her knees, she hugged the wolf close. "Thank goodness you're okay. I can't see a thing!"

"We have to get out of the storm."

"Can you sense the others?" Adriane asked hopefully.

"No."

"What about the portal we fell through?"

"There's nothing here now. We have to move. I sense danger."

Adriane quickly turned, trying to see through the blinding storm. "Which way?"

"We must move towards the mountains."

"Okay. Let's go." She got to her feet and pulled the cuff of her sweater up to expose the wolf stone on her right wrist. She concentrated. Instantly, the stone flared to life, casting a golden glow against the haze of ice and snow. The pair moved as fast as they could through the wall of white.

"Are we on Aldenmor?" Adriane tried to ignore the sharp cold hammering down.

"Yes."

"Okay, well at least we're here . . . wherever that is."

"Somewhere in the northern coastal regions."

"How do you know that?"

"I can smell brine of the ocean mixed in the wind. The storm is passing over."

Her mistwolf senses were sharp. Sure enough, it wasn't long before the blizzard began to trail away. The fog separated, and the vista in front of them was breathtaking. Towering glacier-covered mountains rose from the rolling tundra, bordered by huge brown cliffs.

Suddenly, the sky rippled with reds and purples. Blues

and greens appeared. The entire sky seemed full of color and motion. Then, after several seconds, everything faded to a warm orange glow.

"What was that?" Adriane asked.

Storm sniffed the air. *"Wild magic."*

Sounds of crashing surf seeped through the wind. Gulls skimmed the dunes that ran not fifty yards from where they stood.

Adriane turned in a slow circle hoping to catch a glimpse of Emily, Kara, Lyra, or Ozzie. She scanned the wide plateau they had crossed, but all she saw was stark white landscape battered by cold winds.

Storm growled. *"Something is hunting."*

Adriane bit her lower lip. She'd been hunted once before on Aldenmor. Creatures had used her magic jewel to track her. Quickly, she covered the bracelet with her sleeve.

"Can you reach the mistwolves?" she asked Storm.

The mistwolf looked out beyond the giant ice mountains and closed her eyes. Adriane strained to hear a response from the wolf pack, but only the wind echoed in her ears.

"Help!"

Adriane spun toward the dunes.

Storm's ears pricked up. *"The hunters have found prey."*

"Help us!"

The call came again, this time more frantic. And then another sound. The unmistakable cry of an animal in pain.

Adriane and Storm took off toward the cry. The icy terrain was slippery, but they were swift and sure. They moved quickly, carefully picking their way up the shell-strewn dunes. Adriane crouched and eased herself toward the crest—and looked over.

She caught a quick glimpse of rocky beach and ice-covered water before the thing was on her.

A wave of fur and teeth swept over the dune, roaring like a hurricane. Startled, Adriane fell back, tripping over loose shale. It was the fall that saved her as a razor-clawed paw swept the air where she had been a second before. Big as a bear with piercing eyes black as coal, the snow creature stood on massive hind legs, its matted white fur thick with congealed mud and dirt. Adriane rolled into a fighting stance. Suddenly, the creature vanished, hammered by a roaring rush of silver-furred fury.

Adriane jumped over the ridge and skidded to the bottom. The snow creature rolled across the stone-covered beach, struggling to remove the mistwolf from its back.

"Storm!"

Three other snow monsters turned at once, looking up from the shallow waters of the wide bay. They were using their sharp, long claws to drag a large sea creature out of the waves and onto the frozen shore. Hazy sun reflected off emerald scales as the huge animal thrashed in the shallow water. It was the size of a whale but much sleeker, with tremendous flippers that it used to slap its attackers. Gills along its sinewy neck opened and closed, fanning desperately for air. A long slash just below its dorsal leaked red into the crystal-blue waters.

Confident their prey was sufficiently wounded, the snow monsters abandoned the scaled sea beast and moved toward the dunes.

Adriane chanced a quick look up the beach and saw the first attacker lying motionless. Storm has nowhere to be seen. With a roar, the monsters raced toward Adriane.

"I think I got their attention," she whispered, sweeping her right arm into the air. Her damp sweater fell away exposing the wolf stone wild with bright amber light.

The creatures slowed at the sight, then fanned out to box in the intruder.

She eyed the bear creatures and settled on the one in the middle, a huge mass of fur and teeth. She'd take him out first.

Magic fire flew from her jewel and whipped out in a golden ring. Instantly, the ring circled the giant bear. It leaped back in fright, trying to rip away the fire. The others skidded to a stop, unsure how to deal with this new situation.

Adriane stepped forward, whipping concentric rings of fire into the air, trying her best to make a fearsome display. Before the creatures could decide what to do, a terrifying growl erupted behind them—a silver mistwolf.

Lips pulled back to reveal fierce razor teeth, ears flat, Storm was ready to spring.

The monsters decided to abandon their prey for the moment, slinking down the beach, then moving behind the dunes.

Adriane turned to the sea creature they'd attacked. During the fight, it must have managed to work itself into the surf. With a final painful cry and what looked like a wave of its flipper, it dove beneath the waves.

Adriane and Storm stood together on the windswept shore. Before them was a vast ocean strewn with ice. It stretched as far as the eye could see. Waves tipped with froth churned against the large ice floes.

"We surprised them, but they'll be back," Storm said, catching the worry in Adriane's dark eyes.

"Suggestions?"

"We have to get to Mount Hope." The mistwolf pointed her nose south. *"It's a long trek."*

Suddenly, geysers of water erupted off shore. With gruff snorts, four sea creatures broke the surface. Giant green dragonlike heads with large slitted golden eyes stared at the girl and wolf. But Adriane's gaze was drawn to what sat upon their backs. Green-skinned with long flowing kelplike hair, they stared at Adriane and Storm.

"You there!" A young man called from the back of his sea dragon. He looked to be sixteen or seventeen, but it was hard to tell.

"Who are you? What are you doing here?" Adriane asked, astonished.

"Waiting," he answered.

"For what?"

"You."

5

"HERE, TRY THIS." Ozzie emerged from the thick bushes and handed Emily a paw full of red berries. "Bubbleberries. Should settle your tummy."

"How do you know they're safe to eat?" Uncertainly, Emily looked at the small berries in her hands.

"*SpooF!*" Ozzie spit out a slew of berries. "Quick! Is my tongue green?" He stuck out a red tongue.

"No."

"Good. Then they're okay." He went back to stuffing his mouth. "I used to pick these all the time when I was younger. They grow all over the Moorgroves."

Broken sunlight dappled through boughs of tall tree-tops. Emily and Ozzie walked along a wide road they'd discovered soon after arriving in the Moorgroves, a dense forest region covering an immense area of Aldenmor. Even though the sun shone overhead, they could see twin moons, Della and Orpheus, rising just above the horizon.

"If we stay on the road, we'll end up somewhere," Ozzie said, munching away.

"Arahoo Wells, Dumble Downs, Billicontwee. I was going to visit my cousins, Crusp and Tonin, in Dumble Downs that night I ran into the Fairimentals."

"Is the Fairy Glen somewhere in the Moorgroves?" Emily asked.

"Could be. There's a portal near Dream Lake, I remember that."

No one had heard from the Fairimentals for weeks until that Firemental had come for the girls.

"As long as we don't wander into the Misty Marshes, we should be okay," Ozzie said, looking up worriedly at Emily. "How are you feeling?"

"Better," Emily answered bravely, rubbing at her wrist. As soon as they had arrived in the thick forests, she knew something wasn't right. Dancing shadows moved across the road, making her feel dizzy and feverish. Her clothes clung, heavy with sweat, her mind seemed thick and foggy. And her stomach churned, threatening to empty her breakfast on the trail.

Trying to keep focused, she asked, "So you really grew up near here?"

"The Moorgroves border elf country. My village of

Farthingdale is on the eastern Grassy Plains in the most beautiful rolling hills full of wildflowers. Wait till you see!"

"But we haven't seen anyone since we started on this road," Emily said, observing patches of open hills through the forests.

Shadows skimmed the ground fading into the woods.

"We're sure to spot someone, and they can tell us how to find someone who knows someone who knows how to get to Mount Hope—" Ozzie looked behind him, suddenly aware he'd been talking to himself.

Emily had stopped, rubbing at her wrist.

"What?" Ozzie asked.

"I don't know. Something doesn't feel right."

Ozzie ran back. "Let's have a look."

Emily pulled up the sleeve of her cardigan. Deep red and purple light burst from the rainbow jewel, erratically pulsing like a dull heartbeat.

Ozzie's eyes widened. "That doesn't look right at all."

"It's hurting me, Ozzie," Emily said, rubbing the jewel harder, willing the itching burn to stop.

But the jewel only pulsed darker, deep purples swirling to green and black.

Emily felt the darkness infecting her jewel. She tried to focus. Think. When had she felt these strange, sickening feelings before? Suddenly she remembered—

"Emily!"

Ozzie's scream broke her concentration. She saw the

ferret yanking at her jeans, trying to pull her from the open road.

A dark shadow passed overhead. Emily raised her jewel to cover her eyes as she looked up. Something huge blotted the brightness. Glistening black wings swept behind a sleek head. It looked like a giant bat with a short hooked beak and red flashing eyes. On its back, a gruesome figure rode, apelike and covered in rough armor of leather and steel. It held a crooked staff of polished metal tipped with a red crystal. A wedge of sharp teeth formed a grin as it bore down on the travelers.

"Run!"

Emily saw the ferret hopping up and down, gesturing wildly.

She willed her legs to move off the road and into the cool darkness of shadows. Dust and dirt flew in her face from the sharp beating of wings.

"Run, Emily!" Ozzie screamed again.

The dark rider skimmed above Emily's head, almost knocking her to the ground. The crystal on its staff flared like a demon sun. Ground, grass, and rock exploded, sending Emily flying past a tree. Coughing and choking, she propped herself on her elbows, trying to find Ozzie.

"Over here!" the ferret whispered as loud as he could.

Emily scrambled over a grassy mound and fell behind a narrow knoll thick with moss.

Shadows circled overhead, dark shapes breaking through the treetops.

"What are they, Ozzie?" Emily was breathing hard, pulling twigs from her curly red hair as she hunkered half buried in ferns.

"Goblin riders. This is bad. What are they doing in the Moorgroves—*oh, no!*"

Emily capped her hand over the ferret's mouth. "Shhhh!"

"*Garg*—don't you understand?" the ferret asked, pushing her hand away. "The

Fairimentals have protected this part of Aldenmor for years. Now that they're gone everyone here is in danger!"

"Where should we go?"

"We can't stay here. We have to find the elves!"

Emily's jewel had cooled to a dim glow but still swirled with maroon and black.

She closed her eyes, willing herself to cleanse the jewel. To feel something pure and good—but all she felt was the familiar sickening poison, seeping with darkness.

"Ozzie, I feel something."

"What?"

"It's . . . I think . . . maybe . . . it's—"

"What, what?"

"Black Fire," she said finally.

"*Gah!* Where?"

"Not far. Over that way." Emily pointed toward a thicket of golden trees.

Ozzie was on his feet, pulling at her arm. "Can you make it?"

"I think so."

"Let's go!"

They scampered through the undergrowth, carefully picking their way over fallen logs, rocks, and brush.

With an eye to the skies for goblin riders, they quickly made their way through the trees. In the distance they could see valleys of green sloping beyond the forest.

"How close are we to your home?" Emily asked worriedly.

"That's the Grassy Plains. Not far."

They didn't have to say what they really feared. If Black Fire had spread beyond the Shadowlands, Aldenmor was in terrible danger.

Distracted by her thoughts, Emily didn't see the edge where most of the forest floor had eroded.

"Look out!" Ozzie shouted as Emily set her foot down. She tried to grab onto a sapling—but her foot slipped. Chunks of wet dirt fell away as her body hit the ground. She rolled and tumbled down the incline before coming to stop at the bottom of a gully. Arms out, splayed flat, Emily steadied herself and gingerly pushed to her knees.

She sensed them before she saw them. About a dozen small creatures surrounded her, each standing about four feet tall, wearing boots of tanned leather, woolen pants, shirts and leather vests. Each carried a long, sharp spear, pointed directly at her. She looked to see their faces and gasped. Their heads were contorted and gruesome, snarling, and heavily adorned with war paint.

6

*P*INK.

That's pretty, Kara thought, walking upon golden grass soft as snow through swirling mists of pinks, yellows, greens, and purples. She didn't feel scared. In fact, she felt strangely happy, almost giddy.

"Where do you think we are, Lyra?" she asked the large cat by her side.

"I don't know," Lyra replied. *"But we're sure not on Aldenmor."*

> *There's magic in the air*
> *Love is everywhere*
> *All our friends are gathered round*
> *To celebrate the fair*

Singing! Someone's singing.

"Over that way," Lyra said, sensing Kara's thoughts.

An expanse of forest wild with oak and ivy became visible as the pinks and yellows thinned. Excited voices became clear, cheering, whooping, and giggling.

"Sounds like someone's having a party!" Kara said, looking at multicolored lights flashing in the distance.

Come and join the fun
Dancing under the sun
Let's wave our hands
To all our fans
The party's just begun

"Can you feel it, feel the magic." Kara was humming along to the catchy song, skipping light as air as she danced through the mist and into the full-blown fairy rave!

Feel the magic
Can you feel it
Feel the magic
Everyone can't help but sing along

The music pounded, loud and strong, sending an infectious melody soaring over the enchanted gardens.

"Whoa!" Kara raised her arms, swaying to the beat.

Even the magic glade at Ravenswood couldn't hold a candle to this place—wherever she was. Explosions of color seemed to burst from everywhere. Fragrant, buttery yellow flowers, each painted with bright red stars, bobbed to the beat above the dance floor. Blossoms of sweet jasmine and peach filled the air with their luscious scents. Violet primrose and garlands of silver birch hung glittering over rings of floating toadstools.

The music blasted from a stage set upon a circle of tumbled stones at the far end of the magic garden where three performers played.

Rainbow sparkles cascaded gently, making everyone twinkle and glitter. And the place was jammed, teeming with all kinds of magical creatures Kara had never seen before.

"Fairy rave," Lyra said with disgust. *"Don't get too close, the magic is intoxicating, they'll lure you—Kara?"* Lyra looked around for her missing friend.

Kara danced by shimmying big-footed kobolds. She shook and hopped past cute little brownies and hooting hobgoblins. She bopped and boogied with five raucous long-bearded gnomes. Somewhere in the back of her mind a nagging thought told her she didn't have time for this. She should be looking for someone, Kara thought. Some friends. They were supposed to be doing something important, only she couldn't remember exactly what it was. And at the moment, it didn't seem all that urgent. All she wanted to do was rock out.

"Kara!" Lyra called, slinking through the silky, hypnotic rhythm of the music, paws firmly on the ground.

Kara was in the center of the party with all kinds of creatures dancing around her.

Pint-sized purple pixies perched on purled fronds. Fat big-eyed boggles tossed toadstools and drank from thimble-sized cups. Spriggles and sproggins huddled under tables gobbling strange-looking foods. Leprechauns wandered around knocking into one another belly first and laughing hysterically. And darting over all of them, perching on blooms and dancing in circles were vibrant, luminous beings, beautiful gossamer-winged fairies!

Feel the magic
Can you feel it
Feel the magic

Then she saw three performers on stage. They were totally kickin' it. The band was human-sized, like her. The lead singer's long raven hair flowed as she moved and twirled, scarves billowing around her like silky clouds.

With hair of neon pink and flaming red, the drummer leaped and jumped, pounding out the rhythm on anything she could find—including the heads of two overzealous trolls.

Golden-skinned with dark blue hair, the guitar player strummed a strange-looking instrument of burnished wood that flared and glowed under her amazingly talented fingers.

"Woohoo! They totally rock!" Kara yelled, waving her arms, moving to the beat. The music was glorious, filling the garden with the most incredible magic. It was if nothing else mattered, nothing else felt this good.

Kara danced with a pointy-toed, top-hatted, purple spriggle. The fairy creature raised his feet and arms, dancing up a storm.

"Hi. I'm Kara, what's your name?" Kara giggled, giving the pint-sized spriggle her best smile.

"Me name?!" the fairy creature exclaimed, abruptly coming to a stop. "Why, I'll wark ye muckle tarrie!"

"Okaaaay." Kara danced away into a cloud of sparkling wings.

"Ya poof git!" the angry spriggle yelled, waving his small fist at her.

Beautiful silver-and-blue winged fairies converged about her, lifting her hair, tickling her arms and legs. A few beady-eyed hobgoblins dropped into the fray to inspect Kara's backpack. Snickering and hooting, they opened the zipper, diving in and rifling through the treasures.

One pulled out a granola bar. "Ah harg!"

"Gimme, ya booty bogger!" another cried.

They struggled over the power bar, falling to the ground as another pulled out an orange sock, which he promptly put over his head. "Farf doodle!"

"Git, yer pookin muckle!"

There was a loud commotion behind her.

The fairy map—it floated out of the backpack! Sparkling stars winked andblinked inside the orb. A dozen spriggles had piled up on top of one another, trying to grab it, but the orb floated out of their reach. It rose into the air and hovered above the excited crowd.

"Hey, that's mine!" Kara said, easily grabbing the blue orb back into her arms.

The music came to an abrupt halt.

Everyone stopped dancing, frozen, staring at Kara with wide eyes and dropped jaws.

"The magic is with you."

She spun around to face the stage. The band was staring at Kara.

"What?" Kara checked her clothes. "Did I get any on me?"

The flaming-haired drummer leaped from the stage, landing gracefully at Kara's feet in a deep bow. "We've awaited your return, Princess."

The entire crowd fell to the ground, bowing profusely and groveling at Kara's feet.

"What gives? Who are you?" Kara asked the pointy-eared fairy musicians.

"We are spellsingers," the silky siren singer said.

The drummer jumped to her feet, tapping a fast rhythm with her boots, "Maybe you've heard of us. We're Be*Tween."

7

*I*CY BLUE WATERS rolled past the sleek sea dragon as it sped along the surface, leaving frothy waves in its trail. Powerful fins and a long tail skimming like a rudder kept the riders on its back steady and sure. Adriane and Storm sat in front of the sleek dorsal fin. They watched the green-skinned boy from the sea talk to his mount as he gently stroked tapered fins behind the beast's scaled head. It made Adriane think of Zach and the way he had been with Windy, his brave griffin friend.

The merboy's clothes were sea-green and blue, like a diver's wetsuit. Around his neck hung an opalescent star-shaped jewel. His long, green hair was pulled back and tied with several cords strung with shells. Pointy ears peeked from his kelplike hair.

"How did you know we would be here?" Adriane asked the boy, whose name was Jaaran.

"We were told you would come," Jaaran explained.

Adriane noticed the boy's eyes had two sets of lids. She guessed one was for protection underwater. He had webbing between his fingers, and his bare feet formed natural fins of webbed toes.

"Told by whom?" Adriane asked.

"The mistwolves."

Before she could react, the sea erupted. Geysers of water spiraled high into the air around them. Adriane and Storm watched, astonished, as several sea dragons leaped, arcing high into the air and gracefully diving nose-first back into the water. They were amazing creatures. And atop each rode a merboy or mergirl! One sea dragon cut through the rolling ocean currents, swimming alongside Adriane and Storm. It snorted and opened translucent lids to reveal large turquoise eyes.

On its back sat a girl, long green hair flowing in the wind. Like the merboy, she had webbed fingers and toes. A sea-green shell sparkled around her neck. "Meerka sends her thanks to you. As do I, mage," she said. Her webbed fingers formed a fist and tapped her chest.

Adriane noticed the ragged wounds along the creature's side. This was the one they had saved from the snow monsters.

"I am Kee-Lyn," the mergirl said, pulling Meerka close alongside Jaaran's sea dragon. "The beasts caught us

off guard and attacked." Her voice lilted like waves lapping on the shore. "They are not from this realm of Aldenmor. They appeared out of nowhere."

"I know the feeling," the warrior said. "I'm Adriane and this is Storm. Is Meerka all right?"

"If not for you, Meerka would have been killed." KeeLyn hugged her sea dragon's thick, scaled neck. "The sea heals her now."

Meerka turned her eyes on Adriane. "You fight well. The magic is with you."

Adriane gazed into the dragon's deep eyes.

"She is a warrior," Storm said.

Satisfied, Meerka turned back to the sea.

"When did the mistwolves call to you?" Storm asked.

"Two days ago." Jaaran swung his mount in a tight circle as the others slowed to a stop. "The pack leader told us their wolf sister would come under the rain of lights."

Salt spray stung her face as Adriane turned her gaze skyward. Bands of light shimmered under roiling clouds.

"How could Moonshadow have known that?" Adriane asked Storm.

"The lights may be a reaction to the portals Kara opened with her spellsinging," Storm mused. *"And he has the other fairy map."*

"How magnificent to bond with a mistwolf," the mergirl said with reverence and awe.

Adriane nodded proudly. "Stormbringer and I are from Earth. We both run with the pack."

"The sea dragons and mistwolves run the same path now," Jaaran told them.

"How so?" Storm asked.

"Once long ago, there were thousands of sea dragons as there were mistwolves. Not anymore."

"The Dark Sorceress hunts them for their magic," Kee-Lyn explained, her ocean-blue eyes full of grief.

Adriane understood. "I have been in her lair. I know she covets the magic of such great creatures."

The riders looked at one another, astonished.

"You escaped the dark circle?" Jaaran asked.

"With the help of the pack and a boy named Zach," Adriane explained. "I thought there were no other humans on Aldenmor until I met him."

"We are descended from humans thousands of years ago," Jaaran said, "but our home now is in the great oceans with the sea dragons."

It was Adriane's turn to look astonished. The animals of Ravenswood had told the mages that once, long ago, humans and animals worked together to make strong magic. But those were stories, legends of a time long past. This was real, happening now.

As if sensing the warrior's thoughts, Jaaran added. "The magic of Aldenmor grows weaker each day. And with it so does the race of merfolk."

"You also wear jewels. They must have magic," Adriane observed.

"These are the Jewels of the Sea." Jaaran held up the

sparkling jewel from his chest. "We are the select few chosen to ride with the dragons to protect our world."

"And one day we, too, shall be mages, friend," Kee-Lyn added proudly.

"I am honored to be called friend by you," Adriane told them.

Meerka raised her head to the sky above. *"When the lights appear, magic will rain."*

"Magic rain?" Adriane glanced at her packmate.

"It was the last message from the Fairimentals before they vanished," Jaaran said.

The Fairimentals! "Do you know what's happened to them?"

Kee-Lyn's face fell. "We fear for them," she said sadly. "We fear the Dark Sorceress has taken their magic. Soon the seas will suffer the same fate."

"My friend, the blazing star mage, opened a fairy map," Adriane said. "We think the portals could lead to the magic of Avalon."

"So it could be dark or light rain that falls," Kee-lyn replied.

"I don't understand," Adriane said.

"Magic is only as good as those who use it," Jaaran explained.

Adriane hadn't considered that the magic they were searching for could be dark or light. The battle to save Aldenmor would depend on magic that could heal—not hurt.

"You and your friends must find Avalon before the sorceress." Kee-lyn swung her dragon in a wide circle.

Abruptly all the sea dragons came to a stop in the middle of open waters.

"We are here," Jaaran announced.

"You said you know a portal that can take us to Mount Hope." Adriane looked around, confused.

Large ice floes drifted in the distance, and beyond a stark coastline spotted with browns and greens.

With a snort, Meerka pointed her great head into the waters.

"In the coral forest, below," Kee-Lyn explained.

Adriane focused on her wolf stone. The jewel blazed to life with an amber glow. There *was* strong magic here.

She concentrated and the amber jewel grew warm and began to shimmer. When the shimmer became a broad arc of light, Adriane waved her arm, forming a circle. Storm pressed close to her, and the magic bubble enveloped them.

"We're ready," Adriane said.

Kee-Lyn looked into Adriane's eyes and nodded. "The magic is with you."

Meerka rolled her body forward in a smooth motion, and suddenly Adriane was watching the surface light fall away like a hazy dream.

They sank fast, watching thousands of bubbles circle around them.

Below, the immense forest of coral revealed itself, like a jungle across the sea floor.

They dove below towering reefs of vivid orange, red, purple, and blue. And the sea teemed with a cornucopia of colorful fish, plants, and sea creatures unlike Adriane had ever seen—or imagined. Schools of large sea horses swam through swaying kelp, front hooves kicking, fish-tails fanning. Horse heads with flowing green manes peered curiously, watching the dragons and the strange creatures inside the magical globe.

"Kelpies," Storm observed, her golden eyes focused intently on the bubble wall. *"Sea horses."*

"It's incredible." Adriane was overwhelmed by the magnificent beauty. Would there be enough time to save it all?

"Is this where you live?" she asked.

"We live down the coastline on the far side of the kelp forests," Kee-lyn said. "In Aquatania."

"One day we will take you there," Jaaran offered.

"I would like that," Adriane smiled.

The sea dragons banked under a coral bridge and arrived at an immense underwater cave at the base of the reef.

"This is it," Kee-Lyn said. "The portal is just inside the mouth of the cave."

"Thank you," Adriane said. "I hope we will meet again."

"As do we, warrior mage," Meerka said.

"We stand ready to fight or die with our world!" Jaaran raised his fist in a salute. "Good luck, mage."

"We pledge ourselves to your service," Kee-lyn vowed.

Adriane rested her hands on Storm's soft silver fur and drew strength from the mistwolf. Whatever grand scheme was unfolding, she and her friends had a destiny to fulfill.

She was a warrior. And ready or not, she would fight for this world.

Adriane raised her arm, and the bubble moved forward, lightly floating from the dragon's back. With a backward glance at her new friends, she and Storm entered the cave and were swallowed by a burst of light.

8

"WHO ARE YOU?" The figure poked Emily
with a sharp-pointed spear. Its face was particularly hideous, a viper's open mouth baring long fangs
below deadly glowing eyes. A dozen others stood around
her, each face more monstrous than the next. Their
spears were raised and ready.

"My name is Emily. I mean you no harm." She struggled to remain calm.

One of the creatures pointed to her wrist. Her jewel
pulsed with reds and blacks. "What is that dark power?"
it asked.

"She carries the darkness!" another yelled.

"A witch!" came a shout.

"No, I . . ." Emily began.

"Hey, you! Leave her alon-*aggaagaagaag!*" Ozzie's voice came tumbling down the ravine as the ferret rolled into a heap at Emily's side. *"Doof!"*

He sprang to his feet, boldly pushing the spear away from Emily.

"What is this sorcery?" the creature asked, clearly taken aback by the talking ferret.

"A woodland spirit!" someone shouted.

"I am not a spirit." Ozzie faced the creatures. "Take off that war mask, Crusp. You look like a tree wart!" Ozzie turned to Emily. "Are you all right?"

"I think so," she replied. Emily then noticed that all the short creatures wore wooden masks! Which accounted for the scary faces.

The one Ozzie spoke to stepped back, clearly shaken. "How do you know my name, Spirit?"

"Talk!" Another poked a spear at Ozzie's rump.

"Yeee! Watch it, Tonin! Or I'll tell Auntie Melba to whack your elfish bottom!"

The figures were clearly flabbergasted, talking and muttering to each other.

"And the price tag is still stuck on the back!" Ozzie pointed to Crusp's head.

Crusp slipped off his wooden mask. A frightened face with big eyes, bushy eyebrows, and a small nose and mouth greeted them. Masses of curly brown hair flopped over his head.

The other elves removed their masks as well. They

stood about four feet tall, handsome and strong with thickets of long curly hair. Some were clean-shaven, some had neatly trimmed beards and mustaches.

"You know my name. Who are you, Woodland Spirit?" Crusp asked.

"Don't you recognize your cousin, Ozymandius?" Ozzie demanded.

The elves gasped.

"Ozymandius?" Another elf stepped forward. "That elf was whisked away by dark forces. He's gone!"

"Well, now I'm back!" Ozzie stomped toward the shaken elves. "And this is my friend, Emily. A great mage."

"A mage?!"

"That's right, knothead!" Ozzie shouted.

"This is nonsense!" Tonin stepped forward. "You . . . you're a . . ."

"Don't say it! The Fairimentals transformed me so I could find Emily and her friends."

"Ridiculous! You're all fuzzy!" Crusp exclaimed.

"Ozzie . . ." Emily moaned softly, rubbing at her wrist.

"Elven war masks are for decorating your house. No one *wears* these."

"Goblin riders have come to the Moorgroves. We have to protect our homes!" Tonin declared.

"With a spear? Have you all gone looney?"

"Ozzie . . ." Emily said again, louder.

"What!" He turned around. "Oo! What is it?" he asked, running to Emily's side.

"That way." She pointed, her wrist ablaze. The pain was worse, which meant someone nearby was also in pain.

The elves looked at the section of woods where she pointed.

"No way!" Crusp stated. "No one goes there. There is darkness and poison."

"Who's sick?" Ozzie leaped to his feet, brazenly facing the elves.

"Brackie and his family," Tonin said sadly. "The entire farm, herd beasts, even the colgies have been stricken. They are in isolation."

"Elves are infected?" Ozzie was jumping up and down. "You bimbots! She can help!"

"She can?" Whispers of suspicion ran through the group.

"Look, you Elvin wingdip!" Ozzie was out of patience. "Take us to Brackie's farm! Now!"

Crusp looked to Tonin and the others. "All right," the elf finally said. "But if you use dark magic against us, you will both die."

"Nice talk, Crusp!" Ozzie kicked the elf's leg as they started off down a trail. "Coming from an elf that cheated through every game of pushball."

"I did not. You always used a smaller ball—hey!" His eyes widened.

"Oh!" Emily stood but nearly keeled over in pain.

Ozzie was at her side in an instant. "Can you make it?"

Emily's face was covered in sweat. Clearly, she had a fever.

"I'm dizzy . . . feel so weak . . ." she mumbled.

"Hey!" Ozzie called to the elves. "We need some help here!"

The elves gathered around Emily, supporting her. Ozzie had never seen her so weak. "Ready?" he asked, keeping the worry from his voice.

"Yes . . . let's go," she said breathlessly.

"She is very sick for a mage," Tonin commented. "How is she supposed—"

"She'll be okay, just get us there fast," Ozzie said.

The elves whisked through the thick forests, keeping the drooping girl upright and moving. At the edge of a clearing, they spotted farmland with acres of vegetables and cornlike husks growing in neat rows. A wood and stone farmhouse lay nestled in a rolling hill beyond.

As they crossed, Ozzie saw why the farmland was in isolation. Deep grooves cut through the tall corn, ragged and ugly. Within the grooves, familiar sickly green glowed and pulsed. Black Fire.

Ozzie was heartsick. How could this have happened here?

"The Fairimentals have vanished. We are no longer protected," Tonin said, as if reading his mind.

"Ozzie." Emily pointed. Dozens of animals lay in the grass near the side of the house, covered in green glowing wounds.

The group hurried across the field. Opening the wooden front door, Emily found two elves lying listlessly on beds of reed mattresses. Their breathing was shallow, and their skin glowed sickly green.

Emily immediately checked each one. A little elf girl lay in her crib. Emily would have to act quickly. "The little one first," she said.

"Stand back! Give her some room!" Ozzie pushed the worried elves back.

Emily tucked her curly hair behind her ears, then raised her wrist. The jewel pulsed erratically, shifting from deep red, to blacks and sparking blues. There was no time to think, no time to worry, only to act.

"Shhh, it's okay, little one," she whispered, stroking the baby elf's long hair.

Big eyes looked up at her. "What's your name?"

"Vela," the little elf squeaked.

"Don't be afraid, Vela. Just hold onto my hand."

The small elf hand slipped into Emily's.

The healer closed her eyes—and fell into darkness. Swirling blackness thick as night blanketed her. She fought to stay conscious. The Black Fire had never felt this strong before. It was like a vise locking her in its grip. Here on Aldenmor its power was so much stronger. Overwheleming.

Emily screamed, making the elves jump.

Ozzie ran to her, leaped, and threw his arms around Emily's neck, as if to hold her in place, to keep her from falling. "Hang on," he whispered.

The healer's jewel pulsed with a surge of rainbow

light, slowly at first and then more quickly.

"You can do it." Ozzie hugged her close.

"The ferret is a healer, too?" an elf asked.

"Yes, he helps me." Emily focused harder. She reached for the dark power as it warped and twisted, a live snake in her grasp. But it was too strong, threatening to blot out her jewel, and with it, any hope of healing the elves.

Enveloped by darkness, Emily struggled to find her light. If she faltered now, she would be lost.

Then she felt pressure in her hand. The little elf had closed her eyes and was squeezing Emily's hand as hard as she could. Ozzie's soft whiskers tickled her neck as the ferret hugged her tighter.

Something sparkled in her mind, blooming into a crystalline shape—a flower. A rainbow puff flower! In a sun-drenched field, hundreds of puff flowers glittered, waiting to release their magic.

And in the center of the field sat a huge, purple, bearlike creature. The fairy creature opened his wide round eyes and smiled.

"Phel!" Emily gasped. She grabbed for his magic, a lifeline to pull her from the shadows.

Reaching out great paws, Phel sent seeds of magic spiraling into the air, a thousand lights to show her the way—to lead her home.

The rainbow jewel exploded with light, bathing the entire room in the pure blue of healing.

Emily sent the power cascading over Vela until she felt the little elf's heartbeat sure and strong. Emily pushed harder. She could feel the fever leaving Vela's body, her sight becoming sharp and clear.

The light faded along with her vision of Phelonius, but Emily no longer felt drained. She was strong, whole again.

She opened her eyes to see Vela sitting up and smiling. The sickly green had vanished.

Ozzie leaped in front of Vela. "How do you feel?"

"Ooo, a mookrat!" she squealed, squashing the ferret into a big hug. "Can I keep it?"

"*Gah!*"

A cheer went up from the elves as they surrounded Emily.

"Okay, everyone," Emily smiled, then gently pushed the elves aside. "Bring the animals to the front of the house, one by one. I'll get to them as soon as I take care of Vela's parents."

The elves made a mad rush to the door, trying to squish through all at once.

"She is a great mage," they rumbled.

"I told you!" Ozzie called out.

"What did you do to Ozzie?" the elves chorused in return.

"Oh, geez." Ozzie slumped forward.

Emily attacked the Black Fire with a vengeance,

strengthened with the joy that Phel was alive somewhere on Aldenmor.

Like an angel, Phel had come to her and helped her discover something vital: in healing others, she could heal herself. Emily finally understood. What she feared most—all the pain and the suffering—could be washed away with the beauty of the light within her. Her true path lay in helping—and that was the only true path for a healer.

Finally, all of the sick had been made well.

"We are so grateful," Tonin told Emily when she'd finished her work, "We would be honored if you'd share supper with us."

"We can't stay. We have to join our friends at Mount Hope," Emily explained.

"We'll take it to go," Ozzie called out, still in the grasp of little Vela's strong hug.

Suddenly, three elves ran through the front door. "Goblin riders!" they exclaimed breathlessly. "They come!"

"My jewel," Emily said, watching soft rainbow swirls in the gem. "It's attracted them. We have to leave. Can you lead us to Mount Hope?"

"We can take you to the portal at Dream Lake. If it still works, you should arrive nearby." Crusp turned to the elves. "Tonin and I will take them. You lead the others past the Far Falls to distract the riders."

"Right!" The elf ran out to tell the others.

"Ozymandius, you have changed," Crusp said, facing the ferret.

"Tell me about it."

"No, I don't mean physically. I mean you have changed. You are . . . a hero."

"Coming from you Crusp, that's fine praise. Tell her to put some more grain cakes in there, will you, Cousin?"

"Sweetheart, Ozzie has to go now," Emily gently pried the ferret loose from Vela's arms.

"Mooki!" the little elf cried.

"Hush now, darling," her mother said. She handed Emily a bag of goodies.

"Come back to us, Healer."

"I'll be back, too." Ozzie gave Vela a kiss. "And next time without fleas!"

9

"WELCOME TO THE fairy rave."

Kara was awestruck. She couldn't think of a single thing to say! "You're Be*Tween!" she finally blurted. This band was topping the charts on Earth. What were they doing here?

The lead singer stepped forward. Flowing silk scarves swirled around her. She had sparkling azure eyes and cute pointy ears. Dazzling jewels hung from chains around her arms and neck. "I am Sylina, a siren." Her voice was light as air, soft as a cloud.

"I'm Crimson." The red-and-pink haired percussionist twirled, lightly tapping a rhythm on tiny bells that surrounded her like twinkling bubbles. "I'm from the pixie nation." She wore a bright red jumpsuit and had bracelets around her ankles and arms. "And I believe this belongs to you," she said, finishing the beat on the fairy map before handing it back to Kara.

With a spin and bow, the blue-haired guitarist introduced herself. "I be Andiluna. A sprightly sprite to me friends. Call me Andi." She swung her arm, striking a thunderous chord from her glowing instrument.

"And you are Kara, the blazing star," the raven-haired siren singer said.

"We love your CD!" was all Kara, completely baffled, could think to say.

Lyra stood by Kara's side, tail twitching with suspicion.

"There is no reason to fear us, great protector." Sylina smiled at the big cat. "Kara is perfectly safe here."

"Fairy raves are full of dangerous magic," Lyra growled.

Crimson's laugh tinkled in the air. "Only some fairies are tricksters, Lyra."

A few nosy hobgoblins landed on Lyra's head, hanging over the cat's face. *"Shooo!"* Lyra shook the pesky creatures away.

Kara had a million questions for Be*Tween. "What are you doing here? Aren't you on tour? What is this place? And how come you're all fairied out?"

Crimson hopped onto a toadstool. "Slow down. First of all, we *are* fairies."

"But you're, like, big!" Kara exclaimed.

"Fairies and fairy creatures come in many sizes," Andi chuckled.

"We are muses," Sylina explained. "Muses inspire creativity and imagination, powerful forces of magic."

"But you're all over the radio," Kara noted.

"Number one on the charts!" Crimson whooped.

Kara shook her head. "Okay. Go back to where we are."

"You're between worlds," Sylina said.

Kara looked around. "Huh?"

"As the web grows weaker, hidden pockets of magic like this one are created."

"A twilight realm between worlds," Andi concluded. "Ya follow?"

"Okaaay." Kara crossed her arms. "What about your email? How do you know about our quest?"

Crimson twirled around Kara. "Word has spread far and wide about the three mages. You are quite famous throughout the Fairy Realms."

"Oh, cool."

"Fairies spread magic through nature," Sylina explained. "But it's too dangerous for the fairies of Aldenmor."

"We travel through the realms, calling fairies with our music, helping them restore magic until the web is healed." Crimson beat out a rhythm on a few troll heads.

"Only the purest of magic can make that happen," Sylina said.

"From only one source," Andi added. "Ya follow?"

"Avalon," Kara said.

"Yes."

"But what's in Avalon?" Kara asked.

"No one knows, not even the Fairimentals." Andi swung her guitar over her shoulder. "It's been the subject of debate for years in the Fairy Realms."

"One thing is for sure," Crimson spun to a stop in front of Kara. "It's up to you to find out."

"You know," Andi said with a smile. "You were drawn to us, too."

Sylina nodded. "Only creatures possessing fairy magic may enter here."

The throng of fairy creatures were all staring at Kara. "I'm not exactly a spriggle."

Be*Tween studied Kara intently.

"What?"

"Come, walk with us." Sylina led Kara and Lyra away from the curious creatures. "You are here for answers, blazing star."

"Everyone, back to the party!" Crimson jumped, sending a row of toadstools spinning around the garden. The crowd began dancing wildly around the thumping drums.

Kara walked among cavorting fairies. A little purple spriggle stood, arms crossed, mumbling and scowling at her.

"What's with him?" Kara asked. "I only asked his name."

"It is very rude to ask a fairy his or her name," Sylina explained.

"Fairy names are secret. They are only given as a powerful gift," Crimson continued.

"Ya name a fairy, ya capture its magic," Andi said. "Ya follow?"

"I'm not up on my fairy etiquette," Kara said. "Sorry, little purple dude."

The spriggle smiled and threw himself onto a crowd of dancing boggles.

"Many years ago, humans and magical creatures worked together," Sylina told Kara. "When the portals between worlds closed, some of the magic remained on Earth. Many animals of Earth descended from magical ancestors."

"Some retain highly developed senses," Crimson added.

"Yeah," Kara mused. "There was this dog that saved his whole family from a fire."

"The same is true for humans as well," Sylina said. "Some humans still carry its seeds. Every few generations the magic becomes strong in them." The trio stared at Kara pointedly.

"But I . . ." Kara's eyes went wide with realization. "You're telling me someone in my, like, great, great, great

past was a magic fairy?" She looked aghast at the spriggles and sproggins dancing around the gardens.

"Not just any fairy, Kara. Fairy Queen Lucinda, the
greatest and most powerful of fairy queens."

Kara rolled her eyes at Lyra. "Fairy Queen, uh-huh."

"Everyone knows you're a princess," Lyra quipped.

"That is why the fairy map was given to you," Andi
told Kara.

"Only you can open it," Crimson said.

Kara listened intently.

"Others draw magic from their past, as well," Sylina
said seriously. "One has been transformed and now uses
magic for evil."

"The Dark Sorceress," Lyra growled.

"Yes."

Kara's head was spinning. "This is crazy!"

Sylina walked Kara under gently raining flower petals.
"The sorceress has released a powerful fairy from the
Otherworlds, a hidden realm like this but full of dark
magic. This creature is working for the sorceress in return
for becoming ruler of the Fairy Realms."

"This fairy can appear in many different guises, flowing from one element to another—a shape-shifter,"
Crimson explained.

"A spellsinging master with a black heart," Andi told
her grimly. "And it's after you."

Kara's face grew pale. "The Skultum . . ." She was

suddenly frightened. "But I already opened the fairy map . . . wait, the Firemental said there was another."

"Two fairy maps to find Avalon," Crimson laughed. "That makes sense. Fairy magic is not always what it appears to be."

"The shape-shifter has not completed his work," Sylina warned. "You must defeat the dark fairy and return him to the Otherworlds."

Kara shuddered. "The Skultum is too powerful."

"You are particularly susceptible to fairy magic," Sylina agreed. "But you can use that against him. If you get the fairy creature to reveal his true name, you will be granted all of his powers. They will be your own, and the dark fairy will be left powerless."

"How do I do that?" Kara was beginning to feel way over her head.

The band members exchanged glances.

"Sometimes dance, music, riddles, tricks—the most absurd thing can make a fairy forget a secret."

"What, I'm supposed to stand on my head?"

Andi clapped. "Ye learnin.'"

"But I fell under its power so easily," Kara moaned.

"No demon can possess you if you maintain the ability to turn and laugh at it," Crimson sang in a syncopated, rhythmic voice.

"Easy for you to say."

"That's the spirit!" Andi approved.

They had arrived back at the floating stone stage. Andiluna picked up a sparkling silver fiddle and began weaving an infectious song. The rave jumped back into full swing with fairy creatures leaping and dancing, hooting and laughing in glorious havoc.

Kara watched Be*Tween rock out.

"You have an interesting past," Lyra commented.

"Yeah, everyone's jealous enough of my amazing talents."

Lyra butted Kara's side playfully. *"I wouldn't be so hasty about this fairy princess thing . . ."*

"Hey," Kara said, suddenly realizing something. "If only fairies are allowed, how come you're here?"

The cat stared back. *"Gah."*

"I know how you feel," she sympathized. "Let's find the others."

Kara opened her backpack and took out the unicorn horn. One hand wrapped around the horn, the other on Lyra's back, she called out. "Take us to our friends at Mount Hope!"

Rainbow beams flowed from the horn's tip, glowing brighter and brighter, bathing them in incandescent light. Then the light began to swirl faster and faster until a portal yawned open before them.

"Don't give up the spirit of Avalon." She heard Be*Tween sing as she and Lyra stepped into the portal and vanished.

10

BRIGHT SUN BROKE over the crest of Mount Hope as Kara and Lyra made their way along the dusty trail through sprawling hillocks at the base of the mountain range. Valleys spread below, and in the far distance the broken landscape of the Shadowlands loomed—a blight upon the land. But here it was relatively green. Tall trees led back to the forests along the western slopes. The air was chilly.

"Anything?" Kara asked.

"Over there." Lyra nodded toward an outcropping of rocks near a cave.

Lyra had picked up a mistwolf call. *It's a mistwolf and it's very angry . . . and scared.*

"Where's the rest of the pack?"

"I don't know, but there's something else here. I can't make it out."

Suddenly, a growl echoed across the small path. More of a bark, actually.

Lyra perked her ears.

They advanced slowly to the cave. Kara reached inside her backpack for the unicorn jewel. Brandishing it like a weapon, she eyed the surrounding bushes suspiciously. "What is it?" she whispered.

"Mistwolf," Lyra replied, cocking her head to listen. She turned and positioned herself in front of Kara.

"Helooo," Kara called out. "Who's there?"

The growl got louder. One of the bushes began to shake.

"Odd behavior for a mistwolf," Lyra said. *"As if it's protecting the cave."*

Lyra and Kara slowly approached the scary sounds.

Suddenly, a small dog-sized creature leaped from the bush.

"Ahhh!" Kara jumped back in alarm, then looked closer at her attacker.

It was a furry black wolf puppy with white paws and chest.

"Grrrr-uf!" He barked, hackles raised, teeth bared. He lowered his body and lunged forward with a *yelp*— and promptly fell on his nose, stumbling over too large paws. The pup sprang back to his feet and barked louder.

Lyra regarded the scruffy little wolf.

"Kinda small for a mistwolf," Kara said as she watched the creature.

"It's a pup," Lyra explained.

"Duh . . . hey, little fella,' where's your mommy?" Kara stepped forward.

The pup backed away, snarling.

"I'm going to check out the caves. You keep it occupied."

"How do I—" the little pup bit Kara's pant leg, shaking his head back and forth.

"Hey, those are Calvins," she complained as she shook him off. She bent down and opened her pack. "How about biting into something you can actually eat?" She pulled out a granola bar.

The pup carefully sniffed it.

Kara watched Lyra circle around and enter the caves. "It's okay, see . . . yummy," Kara took a small bite. The pup tentatively stepped closer as Kara held out the food. Snapping it away from her fingers, it hungrily began to chew, keeping a wary eye on Kara. It quickly backed away as she tried to pet it.

All at once, Kara felt a sharp pain in her head and deep sadness seep through her. "Lyra, are you all right?" she asked, worried about her friend.

Kara saw Lyra emerge from the cave. The pup eyed the cat suspiciously, edging back to give the big animal room.

"Mistwolves," Lyra said.

"You found them?"

"Some."

Kara looked into her friend's deep green eyes and knew what Lyra had found in the caves.

"Oh." She looked at the pup sadly, tears welling up in her eyes.

Lyra sharply raised her nose, sniffing the air.

"What is it?"

"Stormbringer!"

"And Adriane?"

"They come."

"Thank goodness. What about Emily and Ozzie?"

"Not yet."

Ghostly mist snaked between the trees, and suddenly the great silver mistwolf appeared, hackles raised.

The pup jumped to its feet, stumbling back on its paws.

"Storm!" Kara called out.

The mistwolf stared at Lyra for a second, then leaped up the rocky incline and vanished into the caves.

"Hey, Barbie! That you?"

Kara whirled to see Adriane walking around the bend along the rocky path.

"Xena!" Kara cried, running to the dark-haired girl and catching her friend in a big hug. The girls hugged tightly for a moment, then abruptly stepped back, embarrassed.

"You okay?" Adriane asked.

"Yeah, you?"

Adriane nodded and saw Storm outside the caves. The

mistwolf's hackles lay flat, her ears laid back against her head.

"Oh, no." Adriane knew instantly something was wrong.

Storm tilted her head back and let out a mournful howl. *"The mistwolves have been attacked."*

Six had been lost to the enemy.

Adriane squeezed Kara's hand hard, blinking back tears, then walked to look over the bluff at the forests beyond. There were no other mistwolves in sight—the caves and rocky outcroppings appeared to be deserted.

"No sign of the pack," Lyra said, confirming Adriane's thoughts.

Storm looked down to find the cub standing between her feet.

"Over here!" Adriane was shouting and waving down the ravine.

"I told you we were heading in the right direction!" Ozzie's voice echoed back.

A moment later Emily's curly hair became visible as she and Ozzie appeared on the path.

"We're here!" Ozzie exclaimed. "Come and hug me!"

"Emily!" Adriane and Kara cried.

The healer raced to embrace her friends. "I was so worried."

"Storm and I were in the Ice Peaks, way up north," Adriane said breathlessly. "We were helped by real mer-folk, and they had sea dragons!"

"Wow, that's so cool," Emily laughed.

"Well, I danced with a sproggin and met Be*Tween!" Kara announced.

"Be*Tween?" Ozzie exclaimed.

"Yeah, cool, huh?"

"You found them here—?" Emily asked, flabbergasted.

"Well, not exactly here," Kara replied. "Be*Tween are fairy creatures. They're protecting all the fairies of Aldenmor."

Emily and Adriane were astounded.

"Ozzie and I were in the Moorgroves," Emily reported. "I'm afraid the Black Fire has spread to other parts of Aldenmor."

Emily heard barking and growling. "Who's Storm's friend?" she asked. The little wolf was on its back, batting away Storm's playful paws.

"His name is Dreamer," Storm started. *"His parents run with the spirit pack now."*

Emily's face fell. "Hello there, little one." Dreamer let Emily scratch him behind the ears and rub his tummy. "Where are the others, Storm?"

"I don't know. But I sense something . . ." She sniffed the air suspiciously.

"Well, at least we're all together," Kara said. "I got all kinds of news from Be*Tween."

"They're not shape-shifters are they?" Adriane asked sarcastically.

"No, but they are fairies, real magical stuff. And they

know all about our quest. We're famous in the Fairy Realms." Kara swept her hair over her shoulder.

"Really?" Emily asked.

"Yeah, that's great." Adriane eyed the wolf pup, then turned to the others. "Maybe we should get the d-flies to phone Zach. Something's wrong. He should have been here."

"I *am* here!" a familiar voice called from the other side of the ravine. On a high ridge nearby stood a cute boy in a white shirt, beige pants, and sandals.

Adriane gasped. "Zach! Have you been here the whole time?"

"Over here, come quickly!" He disappeared behind the ridge.

"Come on," Adriane took off in a run.

The others followed.

"Something doesn't smell right." Storm sniffed the air.

"There is strong magic nearby." Lyra scanned the empty hills.

"Yes, mistwolf magic!"

"Hurry!" Adriane called to her friends as she ascended the rise.

At the top, she peered down at the boy. He stood in a grassy field, waving for her to join him. "Here! I have something to show you!"

"Zach, what's up?" Adriane asked worriedly. Heat bit at her wrist. The wolfstone pulsed with danger.

The others crested the hill and started down into the valley.

Adriane ran toward Zach, but skidded to a stop about ten yards away. Fear tingled up her spine. Her stone was blazing. She looked closely at the strange shimmer cascading around the boy.

Adriane whipped around. "No!" she screamed at her friends. "Go back!"

"Adriane!" Storm snarled, leaping down the hill, teeth bared.

The hair along Lyra's back rose and a low growl rumbled in her throat.

Dark clouds of mist seemed to fill the valley as if out of thin air.

The mist fell away, and the valley was completely full. Dozens of huge, horrid night stallions snorted fire, training red eyes on the trapped group. On their backs sat armored goblins, fierce and deadly. And behind them stood short, black as ink, faceless imps, at least one hundred strong.

Adriane watched in horror as Zach walked right up to the goblin leader atop the biggest and most frightening of the night stallions. The boy's eyes narrowed to evil yellow slits, then glowed blood red. His body seemed to melt as it morphed into a shadowy lizard form. The creature vanished behind the attackers.

"Zach, no," Adriane said, feeling tears threaten to fall.

"How is that possible?" Ozzie asked. "They appeared out of nowhere—like the mistwloves."

"They are using the magic of the mistwolves," Storm growled. *"The pack has fallen."*

"Form a circle!" Adriane shouted, her jewel sparking to fire.

Trying to stop shaking, Emily, Adriane, and Kara stood back to back, facing the impossible enemy.

Storm, Lyra, and Ozzie surrounded the trio, ready to sacrifice themselves to protect their friends. Dreamer stood between Storm's front feet, growling and barking.

"Kara, stand between us," Adriane ordered, moving Kara. "Focus, Kara! We hit the lead riders first!"

The imps stood their ground as the goblin riders approached.

"There's too many!" Kara screamed.

"Kara, the horn!" Emily reminded her urgently.

"Oo!" Kara reached into her pack and removed the unicorn horn. Diamond magic flared to life.

The lead goblin raised a clawed fist and pulled his fierce steed to a halt. "You will come with us either way," it hissed.

"Leave us alone!" Adriane called out. "Or you'll regret it!"

The goblin sneered with a deathlike grin.

"The imps!" Storm roared.

Electrical sparks danced in the air as the imps swarmed

at the group from all sides. Flashing blue crackled along wide nets strung between them.

They were hopelessly outnumbered.

"Don't be afraid," Ozzie said to his friends.

"Emily," Kara said, terrified as she pushed the horn into the red-haired girl's hands.

"Hold it up, Kara!" Emily pressed it back toward Kara.

Trembling, the blazing star held the unicorn horn as high as she could.

"Lorelei!" The three girls called upon the magic of the unicorns. "Protect us!"

The sky exploded with fire.

The girls shielded their faces from the intense heat as flames flew overhead.

But it was not the fire born of magic jewels.

It was the fire of a tremendous winged creature, a flying monster.

The huge beast swooped in, its massive wings cutting through the smoke and flames, making it hard to see exactly what it was.

"Oh, no!" Emily exclaimed.

"The manticore!" Kara screamed.

There was nowhere to go. They were completely surrounded. The magic of the horn had failed them.

11

PANDEMONIUM ERUPTED IN the field. Blue lightning flashed as shadowy imps scurried through plumes of smoke. Screams, yells, snorts, and roars added to the chaos.

"Stay together!" Adriane commanded, swinging her arm, tearing swatches of bright gold light through the smoldering haze.

The girls remained in position, jewels glowing and ready.

"Hey! They're running away!" Kara pointed.

The imps sparked with blue electricity as they retreated, their nets in tatters.

Ozzie jumped up and down shaking his fist. "And don't come back—uh-oh."

But the imps had only retreated behind the leading edge of goblin riders. Night stallions reared, snorting flames, adding to the thick smoke flowing across the field. The riders held bright red staffs high as they bore down on the group, coming in fast.

Kara held up the unicorn horn as Emily and Adriane gripped Kara's hands. Gold and blue flew from the rainbow jewel and the wolf stone, swirling into the horn.

Adriane pointed the unicorn horn at the ground in front of the incoming riders. Magic exploded forth. Four night stallions were blown off their feet, their riders flying as grass and dirt rained everywhere. Six more jumped the smoking fissure, lightning firing from their riders' staffs.

Adriane and Storm leaped into the fire's path, spinning a shield of sparkling gold. Mistwolf and warrior worked like a fine-tuned machine, whirling to block every bolt, sending them flying harmlessly into the air.

But the night stallions were strong and fast, thundering past Adriane straight toward Emily and Kara.

Another group attacked from the side, driving the healer and blazing star apart.

"Stay together!" Adriane ordered.

"Kara, look out!" Emily screamed.

A wave of imps ran between the riders and threw a sparking net over Kara.

Adriane leaped and spun, fists of golden fire slicing the nets to shreds.

Dreamer barked as he ran between the mages' legs, barreling over Ozzie.

The girls scrambled together as another group of riders charged.

Roaring, Lyra pushed the girls behind her, teeth bared, wings unfurled, ready to absorb the crushing impact.

A huge red tail swept through the haze, knocking the goblins off their mounts. The mutant horses careened out of control, missing the group by yards. Emily and Kara felt their fiery breath as they passed.

The creature landed in front of the girls roaring defiantly at the goblins and imps. The attacking hoard dispersed over the far ridge, leaving the group, for now.

"That's not the manticore!" Ozzie exclaimed.

"What is it?" Emily asked, trembling.

The fierce creature turned a horselike head on its long sinewy neck. It was as big as a bus with a long tail covered in glimmering red scales. Large reptilian eyes narrowed dangerously as it snorted. With a rush, it stomped toward them on massive hind legs.

Something opened inside Adriane's mind. Something familiar, strong, and right—feelings of love rushed through her mind and body, it was like . . . coming home.

"Dragon!" Ozzie screamed.

Kara grabbed for Emily's and Adriane's hands.

"No, wait!" Adriane cried.

The dragon lumbered toward them, practically stumbling on his enormous feet. When it was only a few feet

away, it stopped, folding its shimmering, iridescent wings. Smoke drifted from its nostrils as it leaned forward, opened its huge mouth—

"Momma!"

—and licked Adriane so hard, she was lifted several feet into the air.

"Drake?" Adriane laughed as she landed on the ground. "It *is* you!" She threw her arms around Drake's neck, hugging the dragon as tight as she could. Then she stepped back to look him in the eye. "Wow. You've really grown!"

The dragon was happily shuffling back and forth from foot to foot, tongue lolling out. *"Momma! Momma!"*

Thud!

The ground shook as Drake rolled over onto his back, legs and arms akimbo, waiting for Adriane to scratch his belly.

"Tickle!"

Adriane giggled, reaching over to rub the great creature's amazingly soft belly. "I missed you so much!"

The group watched, mouths opened in stunned silence.

"Well, now I've seen everything!" Ozzie stomped over to inspect the dragon.

Emily smiled. "It's Adriane's baby dragon."

"Some baby," Kara muttered as she nervously scanned the skies. For all she knew, full-sized dragons traveled in packs like the pesky dragonflies. She could *not* handle another fan club—especially not one with members as big as the Drake.

"Don't worry," Lyra told her, reading her mind. *"The red dragons hatch only once every thousand years."* She eyed Adriane and Drake. *"He's imprinted on Adriane."*

"Everybody, this is Drake." Adriane introduced the dragon to her friends.

"Hello!" Drake snorted, sitting up. The dragon's lips parted, revealing rows and rows of razor-sharp teeth. Kara hoped it was a smile.

"Dragons grow very quickly," Storm observed.

"You can say that again," Kara replied.

Adriane first met Drake when he was still inside his egg. When she left Aldenmor, he'd barely hatched. She knew that dragon magic was incredibly powerful, but she never expected her friend to grow so fast.

"Such a sweet boy," Adriane cooed, playfully scratching Drake under his chin. The dragon laughed, shooting sparks out his nostrils. A small fireball shot out of his mouth.

Emily, Kara, and the others leaped back.

"AhH!" Ozzie shouted. "Try to keep it on low flame!"

"Sorry." Drake hung his head over Adriane's.

"Drake, where's Zach?" Adriane suddenly realized Drake had flown in by himself. She tried to keep the worry out of her voice.

"He went after Moonshadow and the mistwolves," Drake

replied. He sounded worried himself. *"Zach told me to stay outside so witch would not capture me."*

"Wait, if that wasn't Zach, then who—oh." Kara flashed on Be*Tween's warning about the Skultum.

"That wasn't Zach, and I'll give you two guesses who it *really* was," Adriane said grimly.

"That means Zach is captured, in a spell somewhere," Emily said.

"I have not heard from Zach at all," Drake admitted. *"Then I heard Momma and came here."*

"The Dark Sorceress has the mistwolves," Storm said. *"That is the only way she could be using their magic."* Dreamer snarled.

"But how is that possible, Storm?" Adriane asked.

"I do not know. It takes very strong magic to capture or kill a mistwolf," Storm said.

Drake nodded, shuffling on his huge feet again. *"Have not heard from Zach!"*

"If she has Moonshadow," Adriane figured, "then she has his fairy map. And she must be using it to open the portals."

"The map was given to Moonshadow," Storm insisted. *"He would guard that map with his life."*

"Perhaps he doesn't have the strength to prevent it," Lyra said quietly.

There was a long moment of silence as the group considered this sobering thought—and another that nobody wanted to say aloud: maybe Moonshadow *had* defended the map with his life.

"They tried to capture Kara." Ozzie paced. "Why? What has she got?"

"This." Kara held out her backpack. "No, I mean, this!" she removed the fairy map. "Be*Tween told me the Skultum would come after me."

"Why does she still need Kara's fairy map?" Emily asked.

"We stopped the Skultum before he finished his job," Adriane stated.

"The sorceress still can't find Avalon," Ozzie said.

"So . . . I didn't open all the portals," Kara concluded.

"It's possible," Storm said.

Adriane sighed. "Anything is possible."

The three girls looked at one another but didn't speak. They didn't have to. They were all thinking the same thing. Anything was possible, but their task here on Aldenmor felt totally impossible. And they still didn't have any real answers. Just possibilities.

"One thing is for sure," Adriane finally said. "We have to go after Zach and the mistwolves."

"Well, we can't sit around here," Ozzie agreed. "Those goblins will be back any second. Probably with some orcs or worse!"

"We can't just waltz into the dark circle, either," Kara pointed out.

"She already knows we're here," Storm said.

"So if we can get into the lair before those riders and imps regroup, maybe we have a chance!" Adriane hit her palm with a fist. "We have to move fast."

"Okay, but that's gotta be, like, miles from here." Kara gazed toward the desolate plains beyond the valleys. "How are we going to get there before the monsters attack us again?"

Adriane smiled and patted the dragon's neck. "Welcome to Air Drake."

"Oy, why did I think you were going to say that?" Ozzie groaned.

12

*T*HEY SLID OFF the Drake's back as the dragon landed smoothly behind a large dune overlooking the Shadowlands. Lyra set down alongside, her magic wings folding and disappearing with a soft glow.

"This is it?" Kara asked incredulously.

It was hard to believe that this burnt-out desert had once been lush, vibrant, and full of life. It was even harder to believe that the small band of travelers had any hope of restoring it.

Three girls, cat, mistwolves, ferret, and dragon peered over the gray ridge. Steam hissed across the barren landscape before them. Several ominous structures rose from the sand like smokestacks. Sparks of light flicked and danced from the open funnels.

"We have to go in there?" Kara exclaimed.

"*Some of us have already been inside*," Lyra rumbled.

Kara stroked her friend's back, smoothing her raised hackles.

"There," the warrior pointed.

A stone courtyard led to a pair of black doors at the first tower.

"That's her lair?" Ozzie asked.

"*There's more*," Lyra growled. "*Below*."

The Dark Sorceress's lair lay largely hidden underground. Adriane and Lyra were well aware of the vast caverns and catacombs that wormed under the surface.

Adriane felt her stomach tighten, and a trickle of sweat trailed down her neck. She was back to a place out of her worst nightmares, a place she thought she'd never return to. And yet, here she was. The last time she had barely escaped, and that was with the help of the entire pack. Where were the mistwolves now?

Storm sensed her friend's dread. "*Stay focused, warrior. Turn fear to strength. Use it.*"

"What's that, Storm? Those weren't here before." Adriane pointed to three triangular crystals that pierced the ground in the center of the towers.

"Zach told us she was building those," Emily reminded them.

"That's where she's going to store the magic," Ozzie said.

The squirming wolf pup in Emily's arms sniffed the air and barked.

"Shhh. We have to be very quiet," Emily said, putting the pup on the ground.

"Good point, Dreamer." Kara's gaze was on the entrance to the lair. "How do we get past those?"

Tall serpentine guards walked in groups out of the doors, each holding long staffs. Around the base of the distant funnel, goblin riders rode patrol. Their night stallions snorted as the goblins on their backs scowled into the distance.

"Won't be long before they sense us," Lyra warned.

Kara sucked in her breath. "Okay, so, what's the plan?"

"We go in, then find Zach and the mistwolves," Adriane said.

"Right," Kara nodded. "So we don't have a plan."

"We keep moving forward," Adriane responded.

"Cannot hear Zach!" Drake's voice echoed loudly in everyone's head.

Adriane looked into the dragon's deep crystalline eyes. They swirled in distressed shades of red and orange. "We need you to help us, Drake."

The dragon's eyes lit up with greens and blues. *"Yes, I help Zach!"*

"Yes. But you have to stay out here."

Drake's head drooped in disappointment, steam leaking from his nostrils.

"You have a very important job," Adriane explained carefully. "When I say so, you have to create a diversion."

The dragon looked confused.

"Make lots of loud noise, swoop up and down, and keep the guards distracted."

"I can do that."

"Good dragon," Adriane praised. "Wait for my call. And if any of the others that attacked us show up, let me know right away."

"Okay," Drake snorted.

Adriane reached up and hugged the dragon's neck, giving him a kiss on his wide nose. "We'll find Zach."

"What about Dreamer?" Kara asked.

The little mistwolf stood shyly next to Storm.

Adriane bent low to face the little guy. "You're a brave boy, aren't you, Dreamer?"

The mistwolf snarled and barked, showing Adriane his fiercest face.

Adriane smiled her approval.

The dark-haired warrior stood and faced the others. "All right. We'll take him with us."

Adriane extended her arm. Emily put her hand on top of Adriane's. Kara's hand covered theirs. Ozzie, Storm, and Lyra stood close by.

The three girls looked into each other's eyes. There was only one thing to say.

"Let's do it!" Adriane said firmly.

Stormbringer shimmered under the hazy sun. A second

later, her body disappeared, transforming into a thick white fog. Dreamer watched with interest as the silky mist thinned and slowly settled over the group.

From the desert floor, the dark riders and guards fanned out, carefully watching the skies. They didn't notice the swirling haze as it moved into the courtyard toward the open double doors.

The group slipped quickly inside, and were instantly swallowed by darkness.

"Which way, Storm?" Adriane whispered.

"*Down.*"

∞

Cloudy images surfaced in the swirling crimson water. The Dark Sorceress bent over her scrying pool, stirring it with a single sharp claw. She waited for the pictures to clear.

A snarl curled the corner of her lips as she narrowed her animal eyes. A sparkling bubble burst in the pool. When it cleared, it revealed a room filled with three enormous crystals. The life forces trapped within the crystals seethed with powerful magic. Closing her eyes, she focused again. The picture faded as another bubble rose to the surface and a new image floated before her: a ghostly cloud drifted down a corridor toward the vast chamber of crystals.

"You see. It is like I told you." She spoke to the tall,

dark shape standing near her. Her claw retracted into a slender finger. "They have come."

The Skultum's body shimmered and flowed. "These humans are incorrigible," the thing hissed.

"You have no idea," the sorceress replied in a velvety voice.

"The sequence of portals is opened, just as I said it would be," the Skultum boasted.

The Dark Sorceress spun toward the hideous creature, her long robes whispering to the ground like a shroud. "You are a powerful fairy creature, are you not?"

"One of the most powerful!"

The creature's arrogance grated at her sharp senses. As much as she hated this mutant fairy, she had released it from the Otherworlds, and it still had a job to do. Complete and utter subservience was essential.

"So powerful you let the mages elude your trap?"

The Skultum sneered.

"You got the blazing star to unlock the fairy map. But you let it fall back into the hands of these mages."

"Mages," the Skultum laughed, a hideous cackle. "They are merely girls."

"You know nothing!" She snarled viciously, making the Skultum back up in alarm.

"These *girls* have power! These *girls* channel magic through animals!" The sorceress's voice rose in fury. "The very lifeblood of Aldenmor flows through their jewels!

So do not speak to me of what they can or cannot do!"
She shuddered, then calmed.

The dark fairy stood silent, waiting. "The pathway to
Avalon is open."

"There is still one more portal. One that will take me
to the Gates of Avalon."

"Excellent."

"But, my dear fairy king . . . we do not yet possess both
maps." The half-woman, half-animal smoothed back her
silver blond hair to gaze at the fairy map floating above a
pedestal near the pool—the map she had taken from the
mistwolf pack leader. She had used his magic to open it.
But to find the Gates of Avalon, she needed *two* maps—
and the blazing star to combine them.

Both were already on their way.

The Skultum stepped into the light of the seeing pool
and bowed. Reflections rippled over its distorted face,
melting between flesh and bone. "You shall have the
map, my mistress."

"Then you shall have the Fairy Realms to do with as
you wish."

The Skultum's mouth dissolved into a deathlike grin.

The sorceress extended a claw from her fingertip and
dipped her hand back into the pool, swirling the tainted
liquid. The images faded as the Skultum began to weave
its magic.

The creature shimmered and glowed, arms moving in

hypnotic patterns, conjuring, casting. Then, arching its back, the Skultum began to chant a series of guttural, unintelligible words. They jumbled together, echoing in the chamber, a raw combination of animal grunts and melody. The power grew, palpable and electrical in the air. Then, with a wave of its serpentine claws, the Skultum unleashed the spellsong of binding, sending it to the one who would have to answer.

∞

The group silently made its way through a maze of dank, dark tunnels. Lights flashed in the distance. They neared a wide corridor where the tunnel split into three passageways. At the end of one, red flames pulsed with heat as shadow shapes scurried to and fro.

"*The mistwolves are there,*" Storm's voice spoke through the mist.

"What about Zach?" Emily asked.

Adriane concentrated on her wolf stone, trying to keep her magic contained yet strong enough to get a reading from Zach's dragon stone. She shook her head. Nothing.

"Let's find the mistwolves first, then," Ozzie suggested.

They crept along the right corridor, heading into the heat that poured through the tunnel.

They came to a doorway cut out of the rock itself. Beyond lay an immense cavern as large as a football field.

Staying close to the shadowy walls, they snuck inside. Three gigantic crystals towered in the center of the enormous chamber.

"Incredible!" Emily said in shock, craning her neck to see the tops of the crystals cut off by the ceiling. The rest of the crystals were on the surface.

"Oh my!" Ozzie exclaimed, wide eyed.

The girls had learned how powerful their jewels could be. But the magic these crystals could hold was beyond comprehension—

"*Turn back!*" the voice of a mistwolf yelped in Adriane's head.

"Storm?" Adriane strained to see in the chamber, but the blanket that was Storm still covered the group.

"*Save yourselves, wolf daughter,*" the voice hissed. "*Run!*"

The voice was familiar—but it wasn't Storm.

"Silver Eyes!" Adriane cried.

The veil of mist swept from the group as Storm took shape, leaping into the chamber.

"What is that?" Ozzie asked.

With the veil removed, they could see the crystals rising in the darkness. Inside, they pulsed, roiling and churning with murky greens, blacks, and grays. They could all feel them—

"*Mistwolves,*" Storm snarled, making her way behind the first towering crystal. "*They're trapped inside.*"

That would explain how the sorceress could hold

them. Only cages of glass or crystal could prevent them escaping in mist form.

"Storm, wait!" Adriane tried to stay calm. Shadows were moving toward them from the far side of the chamber.

"What's happening to them?" Ozzie asked, horrified.

"Their magic is being drained," Storm said. *"They cannot exist in mist form for much longer, or they will die."*

Dreamer barked and raced after Storm.

"How do we get them out?" Ozzie was frantically jumping up and down.

"Kara, hold up the horn!" Adriane raised her wolf stone. The time for stealth was over.

"Kara?" Emily looked around, voice tight, like it was hard to breathe.

"She was right here a second ago!" Ozzie ran to look down the corridor. It was empty.

"Lyra, what happened?" Adriane asked.

The cat paced, growling low in her throat. The fur on the back of her neck stood up. *"I don't know. Something blocks my senses. I can't feel Kara!"*

"Kara?" Adriane called, panic rising. Things were spiraling out of control.

"Kara!" Emily called for the third time. She was practically shouting, in spite of the danger.

There was no reply. Kara had vanished.

Grinding rocks sent shudders though the stone floor. Emily and Adriane grabbed hands as the ground beneath their feet fell away, plunging them into darkness.

13

"STORM?" ADRIANE CALLED out. "Can you hear me?"

Jewel light flashed erratically across the dark space.

"*Are you . . . right?*" Storm's reply was faint and broken.

"Yes, what's happening?"

"*I am linked . . . the pack. Keeping them . . . from fading.*"

Adriane wanted desperately to be with her friend to help.

"Is everyone all right?" Emily used her jewel light to search the room.

Lyra's magic wings unfurled as the big cat peered up through the open chute that had deposited them. She leaned back, ready to leap.

"No, Lyra. We have to stick together." Adriane brushed the cat's raised hackles.

"Kara's up there, alone!" the cat hissed.

"Can you sense anything, Lyra?" Emily asked.

The cat closed her eyes, then shook her head. *"She is under a spell. I can't reach her."*

Emily stroked Lyra's head and sent as much calm as she could to the worried cat. "We'll find her. Okay?"

"Phoooie!"

"Ozzie? Where's Ozzie?" Emily threw light across the barren room.

Against the far wall, the ferret was stuck headfirst in a mound of dirt.

Adriane and Emily ran across the room and pulled him out by his feet.

"Spoof!"

"Are you all right?"

"How could I be so stupid!" Ozzie kicked the pile of dirt, sending dust flying. Particles hung in the air caught in beams of gold and blue.

"It's not your fault, Ozzie," Emily consoled him, arms around her chest. It was creepy and cold in here.

"We know she's susceptible to spellsinging!" Ozzie brushed dirt from his head and stomped around. "Now she's under another spell."

"You think the shape-shifter is here?" Emily whispered.

"I would bet on it! And we brought Kara right into its

clutches." Ozzie frowned at the dank rock walls. "Where are we?"

"The dungeons." Adriane pushed away the dirt that had broken Ozzie's fall. "Help me here."

Emily and Lyra, working with Adriane, quickly swept away the dirt. A door was hidden behind it.

"I think you found the way out, Ozzie," Emily observed.

"Always had a nose for direction."

"Stand back!" Adriane's wolf stone pulsed with power. She swung once and a wave of golden fire smashed into the door. With a loud *Poof!* the door flew open into a narrow corridor.

The four made a run for it. Soft lights cast pale illumination from crystals imbedded in the walls. Long shadows slipped and curled as if the tunnels were alive.

Emily noticed Lyra gazing up and down the darkened corridor, her green-gold eyes narrowed slightly. Not that long ago, the cat had been held prisoner here along with other magical animals. Lyra, horribly wounded, had escaped. Emily shuddered, realizing how hard it must be for the cat to return to this awful place.

"I sense something," Lyra said as she sniffed the air. The fur on her neck was just beginning to relax. *"Someone's alive. Human."*

Adriane's eyes lit up. "Where?"

"This way." Lyra took off down the darkened passageway.

The group followed, making their way into a wide tunnel that held the prison cells. The jagged hallway was lined with heavy doors, and the group split up to listen at each one.

Adriane took the doors at the very end. Each time she raised her wolf stone to sense beyond the cold metal and wood, she tried to push the apprehension and fear from her mind. The golden glow that emanated from her stone seemed tiny in the overwhelming darkness of the catacombs. Somehow she knew that Storm was getting weaker.

"Storm! Hang on, I'm coming!" Adriane sent a message to her friend.

"Over here!" Emily called out, scanning a heavy door with her gem.

Adriane whipped a ring of gold around the metal bars in the small window. She pulled hard. The others helped raise as much power from the wolf stone as they could. With a *creak,* the door opened into darkness.

They practically stumbled over the still figure on the floor.

"Zach!" Adriane cried, falling to her knees and searching the boy's ashen face for a sign of life. She saw the red dragon stone he wore on his wrist softly blink.

Emily was beside her in an instant, rainbow jewel pulsing strong. "He's in a trance, the Skultum's spell."

Lyra growled low nearby.

The healer wasted no time. She held up her jewel, sending out a beam of healing blue light.

There was no response. Emily gazed down at Zach's barely moving chest. The boy was in bad shape. He seemed too far away to be reached.

"He's been under awhile. Help me!" Emily called out. Ozzie, Lyra, and Adriane pressed around her, concentrating on sending their own energy to break the spell. Emily, supported by her friends, focused her will. Her jewel flashed and Emily felt a flutter of activity. The dragon stone brightened. Zach's heartbeat was strengthening, his breathing deepening.

Zach opened his eyes and blinked. "Adriane, you're in my dream."

Adriane hugged the boy, her heart full of joy. "No dream, Zach."

They helped him sit up.

"What are you doing here?" he asked groggily.

"Rescuing you," Adriane said.

"Guess we're even," Zach smiled weakly.

"Zach!"

"Agghh!" Zach covered his ears as the voice of Drake exploded in his head.

"Ooo, sorry! Are you all right?"

"I *was* . . . yeah, okay."

"Adriane told me to wait outside and make lots of noise when she tells me. I help!"

"Okay, stay there," Zach instructed the dragon.

"How long have you been here?" Emily asked, rubbing Zach's arms to help circulation.

"I don't know," he said. "Last thing I remember, I had snuck into the lair, trying to contact the mistwolves, then—here you are."

"Zach, we found the crystals you told us about," Adriane told him.

"Where are the mistwolves?" Zach asked, his face growing grim.

"Trapped inside them," Emily finished.

"We have to get them out!" He pushed himself up— then slid back down. "Ow, my legs are numb."

"Easy, you have to stay still for a while," Emily said.

A sleek feline shape darted noiselessly through the door. *I can't find a clear way out. I keep going in circles.*

"I got out last time," Adriane said.

"The sorceress *let* you get out to try and lure the mistwolves in," Ozzie reminded her.

"Yeah, you're right."

Zach wiped matted blond hair from his forehead. "This time she got them."

"And Kara, too," Emily added.

"Kara?" Zach surveyed the rescue party realizing they were one member short.

"She's under a spellsinging spell," Ozzie informed him.

"That's fairy magic!" Zach exclaimed.

"The sorceress is working with a fairy creature," Adriane said. "A shape-shifter."

Zach sighed. "Fairy magic. That's what trapped them."

"Why does the sorceress need mistwolf magic?" Emily asked.

Ozzie shook his head. "Magic attracts magic. She's using the mistwolves to draw Avalon's magic here, into the crystals."

"That's why she's been hunting magical animals," Adriane said. "She was after Drake, Lorelei, and now the mistwolves."

Zach struggled to get up again. "We have to get the mistwolves out. They can't survive in there."

"Storm is keeping them strong," Adriane said, her voice strained.

"She's only one wolf, she can't hold onto them for long!" Zach saw Adriane's face go white—and he stopped talking.

The warrior got up and paced. She lifted her stone, sending a silent message to Storm. *"Storm, we found Zach,"* she told her packmate. *"But Kara is missing. How are you doing?"*

"I am with you," came Storm's staticky reply. *"Stand strong, warrior."*

"She's okay." Adriane could not hide the worry plainly visible on her face.

Lyra yowled, trying to reach Kara but to no avail.

"Some mages we turned out to be!" Adriane slumped next to Zach, head in her hands. What were they going to do? They had found Zach and he was okay. But the situation had gone from bad to horrible. Soon it would be hopeless.

∽

The door to the throne room opened.

Caught in the powerful spellsong, Kara stepped inside, unable to resist its pull.

"Come in, child." The Dark Sorceress sat upon her gleaming black throne. Long silver-blonde hair slashed with white lightning streaks fell over her shoulders and down her back. Silken robes glided silently over the stone floor as the sorceress rose and came to Kara.

Then Kara saw the eyes. She had seen them before, the cold eyes of a beast. Vertical slits opened, pinning Kara in their icy stare.

Kara shivered. She opened her mouth to speak, but nothing came out.

The sorceress moved long fingers.

"—me go!" Kara finished.

"Tsk, tsk. We have so much to catch up on, my dear." Her eyes bore into Kara's. "And you must tell me everything."

Kara watched, a prisoner inside her own head, her own body. "Yes."

"Perfection." The witch coldly inspected Kara. "With proper guidance, your power will be magnificent. You like using magic, don't you?"

"Yes," Kara said honestly. She couldn't stop the words, as if they were being drawn out of her.

"I know you do. You're going to show me what you can do."

"Yes."

"Good." The Dark Sorceress smiled, fangs gleaming.

Kara would have run screaming out of the room if she could've moved her feet.

"Well, come on, show me what you have brought," the witch commanded.

A part of her knew she shouldn't—but she couldn't resist. Kara reached into her backpack and felt cold fire. Power raced up and down her arms like a thousand pinpricks. With her eyes locked onto the sorceress, Kara pointed the unicorn horn at the witch. It blazed with light. But Kara could not release its magic.

The witch's animal eyes glowed with delight. The horn flew from Kara's hands and into her evil grasp. The pure light faded, cracks spiraled up and down. With a twist of her wrist, the horn splintered to dust, cascading to the floor like snow.

Kara watched helplessly.

"You know what I want!"

"No!" Kara screamed silently. She willed her body to flee, then watched, horrified, as her sparkling fairy map floated gently into the air. At that moment, another map, almost identical, rose from a pedestal nearby and drifted closer, drawn by its twin's magic.

"You realize only powerful fairy magic can open the maps to Avalon," the witch said cooly.

"Yes, Be*Tween told me." What was she saying? But she couldn't help herself.

"Be*Tween? Ah, fairy spellsingers, of course." The sorceress smiled. "Fairies are tricksters. They are users, like the Fairimentals. They will use anything or anyone to get what they want."

Kara stood motionless as the Dark Sorceress circled her like a viper.

"They told you that you have fairy blood?"

"Yes, from Queen Lucinda," Kara answered.

"But they didn't tell you the rest." The Dark Sorceress stopped to watch Kara's confused expression.

She stared into Kara's eyes. "There is a reason you and I are alike, child. Lucinda was my sister."

Kara gasped. It can't be! But deep inside, she'd known there was a bond between her and the sorceress. She'd felt it when they'd first met. The sorceress had even told her as much—but Kara refused to believe it.

"Open yourself to the truth." The witch's words seeped

into Kara like poison. "Embrace the magic that lies inside of you. And let it out!"

Music filled Kara's head, words so soothing and luxurious. For the first time, she noticed a tall, dark shape standing in the shadows, green scales running along sinewy arms raised in the dim lights.

Kara's arms waved in front of her in patterns she didn't recognize. She was confused at first, but it soon became clear that *she* was beckoning the fairy maps. They responded immediately, pulsing and growing larger as they floated toward her.

Then, with a flash, the two maps converged and drifted over Kara. Fine lines charged with electric energy surrounded her like an exquisite web. Tiny points of light twinkled like stars.

Kara couldn't think. The maps were so incredibly beautiful.

Follow your path, blazing star, the Firemental had told her. Is this what she was supposed to do?

"If you have fairy magic, why don't *you* use them?" Kara managed to get out.

The witch turned away, but not before Kara saw a hint of—sadness?

"I have traveled beyond what I once was," the Dark Sorceress said, then faced Kara again, eyes aflame. "Now, show me the Gates of Avalon!"

Points of light began to flash in sequence, the strands of the web glowed.

Kara fought to clear her mind and regain control. But encircled by the pathways of magic and under the spell-song, she could not stop what had begun. She felt helpless and for the first time . . . totally alone.

14

"*T*HIS PLACE IS nothing but a maze!" Zach complained, frustrated.

The group had struggled along, using all their senses and jewels combined to find the right way through the catacombs. Exhausted, they had arrived at another intersection with tunnels branching off in all directions.

"How are you doing?" Adriane asked Zach.

"Fine." He slumped against the wall. He was still weak from the spell.

"*I have navigated these passageways before.*" Lyra shook her head. "*But the path lies hidden from me.*"

There was a moment of depressed silence.

"Let's rest here for a few minutes," Emily suggested.

Adriane slid down next to Zach. Emily and Ozzie

joined them, huddled close together. Nobody spoke. The only sound was the *pad, pad, pad* of Lyra's paws on the stone floor as she paced, examining each joining tunnel for the correct way back to the surface.

Adriane sighed. Hopelessness washed over her, making her feel even more tired than she was.

"You know, you're so lucky," Zach said to Adriane, then looked at the others. "All of you."

"Lucky?" Adriane echoed. "What do you mean?"

"I grew up alone. I never knew what it's like to have friends. Except for Windy, of course, and now Drake."

Everyone turned to Zach.

"Then I met you." He looked at Adriane, who blushed. "You have the best friends in the world."

"It wasn't always that way," Emily said.

"When we first met Kara, we couldn't stand her," Adriane smiled.

"Really?"

"Oh yeah, she was the self-appointed miss perfect Barbie princess of popularity," Adriane said.

"So what happened?" Zach asked, clearly interested.

Emily snorted. For a second, Adriane thought the red-headed girl was crying. But when Emily snorted again, it was clear that she was laughing.

"She's just so . . . so likable," Emily explained. "She's smart, funny, confident—"

"Pink," Adriane added, smiling.

"Remem—" Emily laughed again. "Remember when

Kara had to talk to the whole school and the dragonflies stole her hat?"

Adriane nodded. Who could forget?

"That look on her face when her hair came tumbling out—rainbow colored!" Tears were streaming down Emily's face. She could not stop cracking up.

Adriane laughed. "She freaked."

"How'd that happen?" Zach asked.

Adriane recounted the story of Kara's magical bad-hair day. "Emily totally saved her," she explained. "She said that Kara had dyed her hair to symbolize the true meaning of Ravenswood, a tapestry of friends." Adriane was cracking up now, too.

"I think the best part of friends is having those memories you share, moments that make you feel so good inside." Zach smiled. "I'll never forget the feeling I got flying with Windy. Always makes me smile."

"I don't see my friends from Colorado anymore," Emily said. "But I still remember hot summer days and the old rope swing that dropped us right in this cool pond."

"I never used to think much of friends." Adriane gave each a shy smile. "I thought I didn't need them. But that's 'cause I'd never met anyone like Emily, Storm, Ozzie, or Lyra before."

"And Kara," Ozzie added.

"Yeah, and Kara," she admitted. "Now, I couldn't imagine a day without you crazy knuckleheads in my life."

"Having friends makes everything better," Ozzie chuckled.

"Like laughing till your face hurts," Emily giggled.

"Sharing banana milk shakes." Ozzie snuggled into Emily's arm.

"Birthday parties," Zach joined in, smiling at Adriane.

"Finding a true packmate." Lyra sat next to Zach who scratched behind her ears.

"Watching a sunrise." Emily smiled, adding to the fun.

"Making chocolate chip pancakes." Ozzie licked his lips.

"Dancing to favorite songs," Lyra said, remembering mornings with Kara.

"Getting a hug." Adriane spontaneously reached over and hugged Lyra. The cat licked Adriane's cheek. Ozzie, Emily, and Zach hugged the cat at the same time, making Lyra purr with pleasure.

The laughter was contagious. It filled the halls, wafting like light summer rain, sending pure magic into the darkness of the catacombs.

∞

The glowing strands of the fairy maps surrounded Kara in hot white lights.

"You opened the correct combination of portals at your spellsinging debut," the Dark Sorceress said in her sickeningly smooth voice. Her robes rustled as she circled Kara, raising her arms triumphantly. "Now, show me the final portal! Show me where the source of magic lies hidden!"

Kara was terrified. What was she doing? Her mind was spinning as she watched the maps. Yet with each star that blazed to life, she felt a connection, as if she were turning another key to unlock the final treasure. She was the center of the universe in a maelstrom of magic. And it was calling to her, building in ferocity, racing through her. The wonderful power, thrilling her senses. She controlled it all! Yes, I want it!

Had she screamed aloud? She couldn't tell. Time had seemed to stop. She had no sense of herself, only of being carried away in the flow of an oncoming tidal wave of magic. Kara felt she would be crushed under its force, sweeping her away from everything she had known, everything that was real.

Suddenly, a strange image popped into Kara's head—Ozzie with a thick creamy mustache. A banana milkshake? That ferret will eat anything! For a moment, Kara's mind was jolted free from the spellsong.

Then it was viciously yanked back.

Kara was blinded. The maps were ablaze in lights as they merged together, magic gathering along the final path of portals. Somewhere a wild animal shrieked. It was the sorceress.

Another image popped in Kara's head. This time she saw Lyra dancing on her bed, covered in her clothes. Lyra, you silly!

Something was happening. Kara could feel her fingers moving. The spell was breaking. More pictures flashed through Kara's mind—sharing a cheeseburger with Emily and hogging all the fries—handing Adriane a bracelet, a friendship bracelet.

She heard sounds—laughing? It was Emily and Adriane and Ozzie and . . . Lyra! They were laughing!

Kara remembered what Be*Tween had told her: No demon can possess you if you maintain the ability to turn and laugh at it.

Her friends had sent her magic and she reached for it, embracing it like . . . a friend.

The spell faded. Kara quickly hid the smile that broke across her face. The Dark Sorceress glared at her through slitted, narrowed eyes.

Can she hear them, too? Kara wondered. Quickly, Kara started waving her arms again. Without moving her head, she looked around for a way out. Then she noticed that the fairy maps had stopped spinning. They now hung in the air above her, but all the lights had winked out. The barren starscape pulsed dully against the darkened ceiling.

The sorceress seemed to have noticed, too. She was eyeing one corner of the map.

Kara followed her gaze. At the far edge of the map, one tiny light moved. It was traveling on the strands, racing nearer and nearer to Kara.

"That's it!" the sorceress cried. "That's the final portal. Open it!"

Kara swung her arms wildly, keeping one eye on the approaching light. It was moving fast, getting bigger. The light was suddenly running on—legs?! No, wait. It was taking the shape of a horse. No! A *unicorn!*

The realization hit Kara hard. The Dark Sorceress had tried to use Kara to lure the unicorn to her once before. Kara remembered how the sorceress had coveted the most magical of all animals.

Now, once again, the unicorn was traveling the web, coming for her!

"No!" Kara cried. This time the cry was out of her mouth before she could stop it.

The fairy maps exploded in light. Momentarily blinded, Kara fell.

She struggled to her feet, blinking. Silken hair flicked across her shoulder, but it was not the Dark Sorceress's tresses—it was a long tail.

The unicorn stood in the room, as magnificent as Kara remembered. White hide smooth as snow rippled over his muscled body. His long mane and tail ruffled like silk. And upon his forehead, his crystalline horn flowed with rainbow light.

The Dark Sorceress saw the unicorn at the same moment Kara did. Her eyes flew wide with rage. "You! What is this trickery?"

The mighty unicorn turned his deep golden eyes to Kara. Waves of emotion surged through the girl, sure, strong, and loving.

Then, in a voice as clear as rain and powerful as the breaking dawn, he spoke. *"We must ride."*

Kara bolted for the unicorn.

The sorceress snarled with rage. Somehow the girl had broken her binding spell! With the strength of an animal, she lunged at Kara.

Kara ducked. With a leap, she was on the unicorn's back, grabbing hold of his silken mane, burying her face in his neck.

The creature gave a fierce snort, reared upon its hind legs, and leaped.

In a flash of light, unicorn and rider vanished.

15

LYRA YOWLED, PACING like a trapped animal. *"Kara's gone!"*

"What do you mean?" Emily asked.

"She's not in the lair anymore. I'm sure of it!"

Adriane and Emily exchanged worried glances.

"Let's not jump to conclusions," Emily said as calmly as she could.

"C'mon, we have to get out of here." Zach stood on wobbly legs.

"Okay, we'll just have to choose a direction and go." Adriane helped brace the boy.

"And end up somewhere worse?" Ozzie cried. "Who knows what's lurking in this place!"

Lyra had stopped pacing. The cat stood stock still.

"What is it, Lyra?" Emily asked.

"Something comes," the cat said softly.

A high-pitched howl pierced the air, echoing through the tunnel like a ghost.

Lyra turned toward the sound. Adriane grasped the cat's shoulder. Down the dark hall, the strange cry echoed. It was coming closer.

The warrior raised her wolf stone, and golden fire sparked dangerously around her fist. "Stay behind me," she ordered.

Another howl filled the corridor, short and mournful.

Adriane crept lightly down the hall, the others close behind. She put a finger to her lips and motioned for them to stay where they were.

The howl turned into a wailing cry as Adriane slowly approached. Whatever had come was just around the corner.

With a wave of her arm, Adriane spun into position. Sweeping her stone before her, she leaped into the darkness.

There was a scuffle and a loud *yelp!*

"Adriane!" Ozzie screamed, running to their friend.

"We're rescued," Adriane said, calmly walking back into the corridor.

Behind her, a small fuzzy head peeked around the corner.

"Dreamer!" Emily cried, elated.

The group quickly surrounded the perplexed little

mistwolf, hugging and scratching, rubbing, and hugging some more. Dreamer rolled about, happily barking and wagging his tail.

"I don't know who's happier to be found, us or Dreamer," Ozzie observed.

"How'd you find us?" Adriane knelt, staring into the pup's large green eyes.

The mistwolf cocked his head. Adriane's mind flashed on quick images: long, dark, scary corridors, the gleam of her wolf stone, a small wet nose sniffing the air.

"You tracked our magic?" Adriane guessed, impressed. Dreamer barked.

"Good boy," Adriane rubbed his scruffy neck. "Can you take us to Storm?"

The pup looked over his shoulder and growled. Then he barked.

"Okay, then." Adriane got to her feet. "Looks like Dreamer here is a natural magic tracker. Don't be scared," she said to the mistwolf. "I'm here now. Take us to Storm."

∞

Kara felt no fear. They were running on the web itself, following the pathway of portals she had opened. Beneath the unicorn's pounding hooves the endless strands shimmered with pure energy.

The unicorn raced faster and faster. Kara leaned forward

atop the animal's broad, smooth back. The pathways of
light beneath his alabaster hooves glowed brighter as trails
of sparkling magic streamed from his mane and tail. On
his forehead, his horn shone brightly, illuminated from
within.

The unicorn drew strength from her, and she willed
with all her heart for whatever magic she possessed to be
given, freely and unconditionally. In that eternal
moment, unicorn and rider became one, blazing forever
across the infinite web of hope, dreams, and renewal.

One question remained.

"Where are we going?"

Reflected from the glimmering stars, glints of fire
played across the unicorn's golden eyes. *"Home."*

He lowered his head and shot forward. In a blinding
flare, he leaped through the final portal and the web
disappeared.

∞

The halls were so dark they could barely see, but Adriane
did not want to use her wolf stone and tip off the sorceress of their approach. Lyra ran at her side. Her feline
night vision helped them keep up with the determined
Dreamer. At least they were going up.

"There's something ahead." Adriane felt her jewel
spark with danger. She willed the wolf stone silent.

They were approaching a series of large caverns.

"I remember this place," Adriane whispered. "There were forges where imps worked building crystals."

But the rooms ahead were deserted, spilling a soft eerie green glow into the hall. Whatever activity had gone on in there before had long been abandoned. Zach felt his way around the wall, moving across the entrance. He quickly covered his dragon stone as it flashed. Lyra sniffed the air, growling low.

They peered into the chamber, jewels splashing light across dozens of crystals. The structures were all cracked and broken, their sharp edges blackened and covered in an ominous green slime. These had to be the Dark Sorceress's failed experiments. Here was the source of the Black Fire, poisonous residue released from the sorceress's attempts to construct her monolithic giants.

Emily shuddered. Every jagged green edge reminded her of an open wound.

Dreamer scurried back, shaking his head as if stung.

Lyra hissed, the fur on her back raised in a long ridge.

"Oh, no!" Ozzie cried.

"*Careful.*" Lyra pushed Ozzie aside as he almost stepped in a puddle of glowing poison. Sections of the stone floor had been eaten away where the toxic substance had settled.

"Stay in the tunnel and keep moving," Adriane ordered.

They made their way to the last chamber, a vast opening in the earth.

"I can feel them!" Zach cried.

Adriane tried to calm her wolf stone. Surely this close the sorceress would sense the magic of their jewels. But her caution fell by the wayside as they rounded the corner and entered the immense cavern—and saw the crystals.

Something had happened since they were last here. The air was filled with electricity. The three crystals pulsed as sparks of power arced between them.

Adriane quickly scanned the room for Storm.

Zach touched Adriane and pointed.

On the far side of the cavern, red-eyed creatures as black as coal scurried everywhere. Sparks of power jumped and raced, leaping from crystal to crystal.

Emily shivered, even though it was hot in the chamber. Something tickled at the back of her mind, pushing at her, growing more intense. She had felt this before—

"What is it, Emily?" Ozzie asked, looking at her drawn face.

"Magic is coming," Emily answered. "A lot of it."

They all looked at one another. This was it. Whatever the sorceress was doing, it was all about to happen.

"Find Storm." The warrior nodded and the small mistwolf jumped onto the shallow floor.

The group circled around the chamber, staying in the shadows at the base of the crystals.

Dreamer barked at Adriane.

"Storm!" Adriane cried. The silver mistwolf stood in

the center of the three crystals. Her body glowed, illuminated by waves of mist wafting into the crystals.

Adriane ran to her friend, throwing her arms around the wolf's neck—and fell to the cold, stone floor. She had fallen right through Storm as if the wolf was a ghost. Adriane scrambled to her feet, confused and worried.

"Storm?"

"My heart soars to see you, warrior."

"Storm! What's wrong?"

"Zachariah, my son" the voice of the mistwolf Silver Eyes called.

"I'm here!" Zach's face was pressed against the crystal. "Don't speak, save your energy!"

Emily carefully walked around the crystal, examining it, touching it lightly, reaching out with her senses as she would a sick patient.

"Wolf sister!" Moonshadow's voice filled Adriane's head. *"Tell your packmate to release her hold on us!"*

"Storm?" Adriane questioned her bonded.

"Brother," the pack leader called out. *"You must not break the crystal!"*

"What are you talking about?" Zach asked. "We're going to get you out of there!"

"No, you cannot!" Moonshadow insisted.

"Why not?"

"We are all infected with the Black Fire," Moonshadow snarled. *"We cannot be released."*

Zach gasped and turned to Adriane and Emily.

"I have held them here until your return, healer," Storm said to Emily.

Emily flinched. There must be one hundred mist-wolves in those crystals! How could she possibly save them all? She could feel the Black Fire swirling, ripping apart the fabric of their magic.

"Healer," Storm insisted. *"You must save them."*

A sudden commotion and flashes of blue drew their attention to the back of the cavern. Dozens of imps had left the forges, aware of the strangers' intrusion. With a wail, the imps pounced like a black wave.

Lyra roared as Adriane jumped, spinning in the air, landing and rolling across their path. She sprang up into a fighting stance, wolf stone raised and blazing. With a fierce swing, she launched a ring of golden fire. The imps in front exploded in inky blobs, splattering across the floor.

Shrieking, the others ran as fast as they could out the door.

"If the sorceress hasn't noticed us yet, she sure has now," Zach said.

Adriane grabbed Emily's arms. "Can you do this? Can you save them . . . and Storm?"

Emily's lips trembled, her heart in her throat. "I . . . I don't know."

"Emily," Ozzie was at her side. "When that magic hits, they'll be killed for sure. You have to try."

Emily looked at her friends. She was a healer, she had to act. "I need time."

"I'll get it for you," Adriane said.

"What are you going to do?" Zach asked, stumbling to her side.

"I'm going to pay a visit to the Sorceress."

"I'm going with you," the boy insisted.

"No. You stay here and help Emily. She needs the power of your dragon stone."

Zach was not convinced.

"Zach," she said carefully. "You're barely healed yourself. I need room to maneuver. I can't be worried about you."

Zach nodded. "I've seen you in action. No one's better."

A twitch of a smile played across Adriane's lips.

"I'll go with her," Lyra growled, lips drawn in a vicious snarl. *"It's payback time!"*

No one was going to argue with that cat.

"All right," Adriane said. "Let's go!" She took a step and faltered—and turned to Storm. She could not afford the emotion. Not now. She stared at her friend. The mistwolf was transparent—fading.

"I am always with you."

Adriane turned away and closed her eyes, letting the feelings wash through her, honing them into a laser beam of purpose.

Without a backward glance, she strode into the corridor. If she had looked back, she would have broken, knowing that was the last time she would ever see her packmate alive.

16

KARA STOOD ON the beach, watching waves rolling lazily upon the warm sands. Before her, giant flat stones with intricate mosaic patterns stretched out across the water itself. The floating bridge led to three stone rings encircling an island offshore. She could make out no details of the island—it was completely shrouded in mist.

A fragrance sweeter than freesia or jasmine blooms filled the air. She turned to see dozens of floating figures. Gossamer wings seemed to catch and hold the light, reflecting it onto their flawlessly smooth faces and flowing hair—fairy wraiths. Large emerald eyes watched her.

"We have waited for your return, blazing star," a wraith of unimaginable beauty spoke.

"Where am I?" Kara asked. But the moment the words left her tongue, she knew. She had been here before. Was it in a dream?

"You are at the Gates of Avalon."

Kara felt a chill run through her body.

"The great unicorn has brought you here." Another wraith fluttered close by, her long silken body almost translucent as she sparkled in the air.

A warm wind whispered past Kara's face, tickling her neck and ears. She looked into the large exotic eyes of the wraiths. Warmth filled her body as voices seemed to come from everywhere at once.

"Close your eyes."

"Now open them."

With a whoosh of sea and spray, the mysterious island swept past her in a dizzying vision.

"What do you see?"

The waters fell away into stars. Golden lines spiraled and looped into the distance—the magic web.

Mesmerized by the intricate beauty of the web, Kara stared as images turned like pages from an ancient book. Deep, rich forests, sun-kissed fairy meadows, crystal-peaked mountains, glittering lakes of blue—she was looking at Aldenmor! It was so beautiful she could barely contain herself.

"Everything's changed," Kara breathed.

Suddenly the image zoomed across the web to another place, a place untouched by time. A glorious city appeared like something out of a dream. Crystalline spires rose against skies of blue and white. Magic sparkled like city lights—a city of magic!

"Avalon really does exist!"

"It does for you."

The images faded as Kara turned toward the gentle voices. "I don't understand."

"You choose to see it."

"As it once was."

"As it will be again."

Kara slowly began to understand. If you believe hard enough, dreams can come true.

"Is that Avalon?" she asked in amazement.

"The Gates of Avalon are locked." The wraith pointed to the mysterious island.

"Only three mages together may enter the Gates," another wraith said. "With the key."

"But I need magic to save Aldenmor," Kara said worriedly.

"And magic you shall have."

"But once the magic begins to flow, it cannot be stopped," a wraith said. "It could be wonderful and it could be very dangerous. Do you understand, mage?"

"Totally," Kara said. "I mean, no." She had so many questions she wasn't sure what to ask. How was she supposed to start the magic? Would it be enough? And where were her friends? Were they okay? She opened her mouth, "What is a blazing star?" she finally asked.

"There are a few who not only choose their own destiny, but change the path of the future. Your power is guiding magic along the right path, choosing what it will become. You are an ember from the fire, waiting to rise into a blazing star."

Kara nodded. She still felt unsure and suddenly shy. "I don't feel special. I just want to help my friends."

The wraiths encircled her.

"Make the magic shine, blazing star."

Kara saw something shimmering at her feet. It was a scalloped, teardrop-shaped jewel—the very one Kara had found in the pond at Ravenswood so long ago. Then, she couldn't keep it, because it had not been given to her.

Kara stared at the unicorn jewel, stunned. "But I returned it to you."

"You have made it yours."

She knelt and reached for the jewel, grasping it in her hand. A spark of light flashed from the stone. A magic jewel! It was everything she had ever wanted—why didn't it seem so important now? All she wanted was to find her friends, to make sure they were okay. She wanted to help save the creatures of Aldenmor.

Kara turned the jewel over in her hands. It sparkled with magic. "Thank you," she said to the wraiths.

The wraiths fell away, vanishing with the wind, leaving her with a whisper, "*The magic is with you, now and forever.*"

Suddenly, there were no more questions. There was

only one choice. Kara pictured magic, pure and good, flowing to a world that desperately needed it.

She held her new jewel high and concentrated. The unicorn jewel blazed with diamond-bright light. Suddenly, the waters around the island surged and swirled between the stone rings, building into waves of energy. With a rush, the whirlpool lifted into the air and streamed across the sky. Ribbons of rippling lights cascaded onto the web.

It had begun.

Kara smiled—and everything vanished as she was jerked backwards, pulled into the forbidden Otherworlds.

∞

The Dark Sorceress stalked across the stone floor of her throne room. Her blood boiled, bubbling like the tainted water in her seeing pool. The blazing star and the unicorn had been within her grasp—right here in the same room! And now they were gone.

Those Fairimentals had tricked her! She had been wrong about the maps. Instead of revealing the Gates of Avalon, the joining of the maps had called the blazing star's unicorn. Now that mage could be inside Avalon—

The Dark Sorceress felt the wave like a jolt!

She watched the fairy map, hanging open like a twinkling dome. One by one, the stars flashed as magic flowed, coursing its way through the sequence of portals, heading for her crystals. She licked her lips with a pointed tongue. She would have liked once and for all to find out where the Gates of Avalon were, but the girl had vanished before revealing the location. It didn't matter really. Let the Skultum deal with her, she thought.

The girl had released the magic—and yet, feelings of uneasiness prickled against her skin. A warning.

Another jolt!

Something was not right. The magic of Avalon should have reached the one she needed to weave a new web. Yet the magic was coming. She wasn't wrong about that.

Had the blazing star opened the last portal?

Gripping the stone pedestal, she reached out, but it was not the magic of Avalon she felt. It was familiar, magic she had never thought to touch again. The sorceress laughed aloud. Here she was trying to build a new key, and the blazing star had just found the original key to the Gates of Avalon!

A striking turn of events!

She raised her arms. Lightning crackled from her fingertips—she had to make sure her crystals would secure this magic. She reached out to tap into the mistwolves—

Snarling teeth snapped at the sorceress in a roar of defiance.

The sorceress reeled back with the force of the shock.

Something was blocking her from their magic!

A silver mistwolf swirled before her eyes, flowing in and out of mist, holding the magic of the pack strong.

Along the fairy maps, star points gleamed and flashed as the magic flowed closer.

Carefully, she dipped a claw into the pool. An image of a red-haired girl surfaced. Emanating from the magic jewel on the girl's wrist was a strong, blue-green light. It pulsed, slowly at first and then rapidly. The light surrounded the huge crystals.

Another of those mages! How had they escaped the dungeons? For the first time in decades, the Dark Sorceress felt something worming its way through her: doubt—and fear.

Furious, she swiped her hand through the water, splashing it across the floor—and over the boots of a tall, dark-haired girl.

The witch stood with a start. How could this girl have gotten into her chamber? Then she noticed the large beast slinking from the shadows to stand next to the girl. The cat's eyes glowed with feral rage and its lips pulled back, revealing razor teeth.

Instantly suppressing her surprise, the sorceress carefully walked to the center of the room.

"Well, well, the warrior mage." A smile played across her thin lips. "I'll say one thing about you mages, you're stubborn."

"And you're dead meat!" Adriane's heart hammered in her chest.

"Eloquently put, but I wish you would learn some manners." The Dark Sorceress raised her hand, and the giant doors behind Adriane and Lyra slammed shut, locking them in the chamber.

Adriane was suddenly aware of the stone wall at her back, and the fact that Stormbringer was not at her side. She didn't see any of the sorceress's serpent guards, but they could be hiding in the shadows.

The witch's eyes fixed on the wolf stone. "I know what you think you're doing, trying to buy your friend some time to heal the mistwolves. But they're long gone." The sorceress's eyes sparked. "Just like your mistwolf."

Adriane faltered, stung.

"Your wolf is dying while we sit here and chat." Her blood-red lips contorted into a wicked smile. "And for what?"

For an instant, all Adriane wanted to do was run back and fight alongside Storm. She fiercely pushed the feeling away.

"And what about you, great beast?" The sorceress sneered at Lyra. "Where's your friend, the blazing star?"

Adriane quickly scanned the room and spotted Kara's backpack on the floor. But her friend was not there. "What have you done with her?" she demanded.

"Me? Why nothing. She has abandoned you. And as you can see," she swept her hand to the flowing lights of the star map, "the blazing star has released magic for my crystals."

Lyra circled behind the sorceress, snarling. "*You will pay for what you have done.*"

"Ah, yes." The witch extended long claws from her fingers. "I remember now. Your sisters were some of the first I tried in the crystals. I watched them struggle for hours. And what did you do? You ran away because you couldn't help them."

Lyra roared in anger.

"Doesn't matter now. Do you really think you can stop me?" the sorceress railed. "You have been a thorn in my side for too long! All of you! Right now, my armies come. And with them my special warrior. You remember it, don't you?" She stared at Adriane. "It's called a manticore. Vicious creature, lethal."

Adriane signaled Lyra with her glance. The cat pounced, lunging straight for the sorceress. With a wave of the witch's hand, red fire shot across the room. Lyra's wings flew open, and she swooped into the air above the deadly magic. The witch followed, trying to hit the cat again. The distraction was long enough for Adriane to hide what she was doing.

"Drake!" Adriane called, raising her wolf stone in the air.

"*Momma!*" the dragon's voice boomed in her head. "*There are many creatures here!*"

"Remember what I told you?"

"*Yes.*"

"Do it. Now!"

"*I help!*"

"Yes, Drake, help us!" Then Adriane leaped. She spun

into a circle, weaving rings of golden fire from her fists. With every ounce of strength she could muster, she forged the rings into a fireball and hurled it at the sorceress.

The witch caught the movement and blocked the oncoming magic, shattering it into the walls. Adriane feinted to the left, sending another fireball straight at her enemy. This one smashed into the sorceress, covering her in blazing light.

Lyra landed at Adriane's side, forcing her own strength into the warrior's jewel. Adriane spun again, building the power, throwing a third ball of magic careening into the witch. Again and again, she pounded away, screaming in rage as wolf fire consumed the sorceress, lighting the room in a rising inferno.

Adriane spun to a stop, breathing hard, exhausted. She had not meant to unleash such excessive force. Save your strength, she told herself. Don't let your emotions cloud your actions!

The tower of fire that was the sorceress blazed wildly. Then it began to move, gliding across the floor. In a sudden burst, the fire lifted from the witch—revealing her untouched.

She waved a clawed finger in a spiraling motion. Adriane suddenly felt dizzy and disoriented. The room seemed to shift as the witch slammed the fire back against Adriane and Lyra. They were thrown against the wall and crumbled to the ground.

Pinpricks of light burst in Adriane's head. Trying to

stop the room from spinning, she saw Lyra slumped on the cold floor.

"That was good. Very good. You know why I am not going to kill you, don't you?"

Adriane watched the sorceress brush herself off as if nothing had happened.

"I'm going to build a special crystal just for you and your friends." She casually sat on her throne and laughed. "I think your magic is quite ready for harvesting."

17

KARA HAD NO idea where she was. Skeletal trees loomed through flowing mist. It was hard to make out much else in the gloomy twilight. The place was eerily quiet, but she knew she wasn't alone. She could sense him before she saw him, and he—the one she had to face—was the real danger.

He had deceived her. He'd made her believe she had talent, that she could sing—and instead tricked her into spellsinging. That set off the chain reaction as one portal after another opened. Now the magic was flowing—so what was she doing here?

"Kara Davies." She finally heard the deep, velvety voice she remembered so well.

Kara turned slowly, and defiantly stared into his eyes,

dark as coal, mean as a winter night. He looked exactly as he had at the Ravenswood benefit concert, morphed into the body of tall, dark-haired, magnetic Johnny Conrad.

"Congratulations." He clapped his hands and bowed. "A jewel. Just what you've always wanted. Pity it won't do you any good here."

Even now, she had to remind herself, this was *not* Johnny Conrad. This creature was not even flesh and blood. This was the dark fairy Be*Tween had told her about. But it didn't matter what shape he took, or what he told her. Kara's fear turned to shimmering anger. No one made a fool of Kara Davies, not even him!

There was only one way to defeat him—make him reveal his real name, trick him into saying it out loud.

Now, dressed in Johnny's signature black leather pants and open-neck silk shirt, he took a step closer. "The blazing star, going out in a blaze of glory," he taunted. "Maybe I'll write a song about it."

"Where are we?" Kara asked.

"This is the Otherworlds, and only one of us will leave." He spun into a dance move. "It's only fitting that we meet here. You see, this is where I was trapped until freed by the—oh, you know, it's all in the family."

Kara would not flinch. There was no way would she give him the satisfaction of frightening her. "By the way," she said, forcing herself to appear calm. "You're not Johnny Conrad. So what should I call you? Your zillions of enquiring fans want to know."

"It's—Ha! Uh-uh," he wagged his finger, then singsonged, "I'll never te-ell."

Kara shrugged. "Have it your way. You tricked me once, but in the end, I sent you packing."

"That's the nice thing about life, isn't it?" he sneered. "You always get a second chance."

Kara held her defiant posture. And hoped he didn't see her swallow, didn't hear her heart thudding.

"This will be so much fun!" He clapped his hands.

"Don't underestimate me," Kara growled. He was so cocky, so sure of himself. There had to be a way she could trick him. He was wily though—and expecting her to try that.

He began to circle her, taunting, "You have no friends here, no winged cats, mistwolves, or fast-talking ferrets—no one to save you. Let's see you spellsing your way out of this one!"

As he babbled, Kara pressed herself, Think! What would Emily do? What would Adriane do? What would the fairies do? She had fairy magic; what did that mean?

"Spellsinging, been there, done that." She shrugged. "Is that all you can do?"

That got his attention. "I can do lots of things," he bragged.

Her mind raced—could she match him, use her wits to save herself, get him to blurt his own name?

"I know," she said. "Why don't we play a game?"

"Excellent." His eyes narrowed.

Kara focused on her new unicorn jewel. She never had a stone of her own before. Maybe she could tap into her fairy magic . . . but what magic did she know how to use? Magic that was hers alone—

Pop! Pop! Pop! Pop! Pop!

Colored bubbles burst in the air. That sound, which usually annoyed her, was music to her ears.

"Kaaraa!"

The Skultum watched intently as five mini dragons flew and chirped happily around Kara's head. "Fairy dragons? Oh, this is good!" He laughed. "No one bonds with fairy dragons."

"Think again, slimeball. I do."

Red Fiona, purple Barney, blue Fred, orange Blaze, and yellow Goldie. They were fairy creatures—the kind that didn't need portals to flit from one world to another. From the start, the dragonflies had been drawn to Kara and only Kara. It was the only magic she'd ever really had on her own.

While the Skultum was trying to catch the fast creatures, Kara's mind was on fast-forward. The d-flies, when she asked them, could form a magic circle and create portable portals, windows the girls had used to see and talk to one another, even from different worlds.

She could make them form a circle, what else could they . . . And then it hit her. If the dragonflies could form a circle, she reasoned, could they form . . . other things, like letters?

As if they read her mind, they answered her! Kara watched, amazed, as Barney flew in a K shape; Fiona twisted into an A, Fred formed another A, Goldie formed an R, Blaze zigzagged into more As!

Her jaw dropped! She whirled around, but the Skultum, still trying to catch the dragonflies, had no clue what the miraculous little creatures were doing! Did they know the Skultum's name?

All she needed to figure out now was how to make him say it. Kara looked up as the dragonflies buzzed over her head. She took a deep breath, and went for it. "Hey, Skultum thing," she called. "Look."

Kara prayed this would work. She cartwheeled—the dragonflies mimicked, somersaulting around her, their jeweled eyes sparkling.

The Skultum was intrigued. She had hit on something.

She ran in a figure eight, they followed, making the same pattern in the air.

Just as Kara had hoped, the Skultum couldn't help himself. He was hopping and clapping, running around repeating their figure eights. Games were his stock in trade.

"Watch this," Kara said, "I can get them to spellspeak."

"You cannot," he said.

"Yes I can!" she responded.

"No you can't," he insisted.

"Betcha! Just watch."

Kara drew her fingers in the air, and formed a T. As they'd done before, two dragonflies—Fred and Blaze formed the letter. Kara grinned, encouraging them silently.

"You try it," she urged.

His eyes lit up, "Okay." Using the forefinger of his right hand, and a half-moon shape with his left, he made the letter D. Goldie, Barney, and Fiona gleefully did the same. "This is too easy."

"Oh, wait!" Kara cried, as if she'd just thought of it. "I have the best game of all. Dragonfly charades. I think of word, they form the letters—you have to guess!"

He threw back his head and laughed. "You slay me, Kara, you really do."

Just wait, she thought. I'm not the blazing star for nothing! She said, "I'll start."

Kara started with an easy word. The d-flies' eyes swirled with excitement as they watched her form letters.

Then with a flurry of activity, the d-flies created the letters using their little bodies.

The Skultum guessed it: "Star."

Kara graciously bowed, extending her arm.

It was his turn. He signaled the motions, they flew into formation: Barney made a circle, Fiona, the squiggly line that finished the Q. "Queen!" Kara guessed what it was before they were finished.

"You go," he directed. She asked for "Flobbin."

The Skultum's next word was another easy one for Kara. "Banshee."

She still wasn't close to what she needed. She needed to make him say his name—without realizing he was doing it. A silly joke she'd made to Be*Tween came back to her when they told her what she'd have to do. Kara had quipped, *What, am I supposed to stand on my head?* It was worth a shot.

"Ooookayhey," Kara sang. "You're right. This is too easy. Let's try it . . . upside down!"

"That's preposterous—" he started, then watched her with glee. He couldn't help himself. The challenge was too, too tasty.

Kara began a cartwheel and stopped when she was balanced on her hands, upside down.

She urged the d-flies to form the letters: DOOWS-NEVAR. The Skultum stood on his head and read it: "Ravenswood!"

His upside down was: GNOSLLEPS: "Spellsong!"

Kara was ready. She snapped her fingers and winked at the d-flies—they knew. "One last word—and this one's for the money."

"One for the money, two for the show—this show is over, and I get to go!" He giggled, standing on his head and watching carefully as the dragonflies formed their last word: DRAWOH.

At the top of his lungs, he shouted, "Howard!"

His jaw dropped, his eyes bugged. Too late. He realized what he'd done.

Bright green magic streamed from the fairy, covering

Kara in light. Now back in its true and horrid form, the Skultum stood frozen. Its reptilian scales glistened as it faded away.

The last words he heard were Kara's: "You won! You won!" Like a Cheshire cat, the Skultum disappeared, leaving only its surprised face. With a *Pop!* it vanished.

Kara rounded up the dragonflies. "Great work, guys."

They chattered and squeaked, twirling happily in the air.

"There's just one more thing I need," she said.

The d-flies stopped in mid-twirl. "o.o"

18

*E*MILY BRUSHED HER damp hair back as she stood in the center of the three crystals. The familiar feeling of hopelessness welled inside. It was mixed with a new feeling—dread. Then Emily felt something else. The room lurched and started shaking. Emily knew what it was. The wave was getting closer, rising into a crest that would crash into the crystals, washing away everything in its path.

"You did it before, Emily." Ozzie stayed close on her heels. "Remember little Vela and the elves."

Emily nodded. She had been sick, her jewel infected with the dark poison.

A hundred mistwolves were infected now. This was different . . . Or was it? She could feel the pull of the

Black Fire, reaching for her. But it wasn't as strong. She realized she had formed an immunity of sorts, a shield. Another gift from her friend, the fairy creature, Phel. She had healed herself and she believed with all her heart that she was strong, she was ready.

Zach stood to her left, dragon stone pulsing with red power.

"*There are too many of us!*" Moonshadow called. "*Save yourselves!*"

"Keep quiet, brother," Zach said. "You sound like a squeaky mouse."

"*A mouse?! When I get out of here, I'm going to show you who's a mouse!*"

"*You* are, that's who!" Zach goaded his wolf brother on.

Suddenly, the crystals began to pulse together in a unified rhythm.

Emily pushed harder, her stone flashing with incandescent intensity. The crystals were shaking and rocking.

"It's too late!" she cried.

"What's happen—"

Ozzie's voice washed away under the thunderous roar as the massive wave of magic slammed into the cavern.

Emily tumbled back, overwhelmed by its power. Cries of agony rose from the mistwolves as magic poured into the crystals, crushing everything in its way.

There was a loud *Crack!*

The base of one crystal had cracked! It forked and

snaked its way upward. Flaming green liquid spurted from the gaps.

"Look out!" Emily screamed, dousing the poison with blazing blue light.

Green droplets splattered at their feet.

"Gah!" Ozzie jumped back to avoid the burning poison.

"Healer! Run!" Moonshadow called out.

"No!" Emily shouted back.

If the enormous crystal blew apart now, the Black Fire fallout would be worse than anything the already ravaged world of Aldenmor had suffered. But if she didn't do something, the mistwolves would die.

"Zach, when I say so, split open the crystal!" Emily ordered.

"Are you sure?"

"Yes! I've stabilized most of the wolves, I'll finish the job as they come out."

"You hear that?" Zach yelled into the crystals.

"Yes," Moonshadow answered.

Without taking her eyes off the first crystal, Emily held out her arms. The rainbow jewel was blinding. "I can do this." There was not a single shred of doubt in her voice.

Ignoring the deafening rumble and the glowing green flames erupting around her, Emily pictured the mistwolves, strong and whole. She firmly held up her shield of light. "Now!"

Zach fired his dragon stone at the crystal, covering it in red. The crystal shook violently and shattered, exploding upward as if hurled from the earth itself.

Thirty mistwolves leaped into the chamber. Some fell to the ground roiling in pain. Others, growling and snarling, tried to shake off the Black Fire.

Ignoring his wounds, Moonshadow stumbled past them, herding the wolves into the light of the healer.

"Moonshadow!" Zach recognized his pack brother at once. The wolf was badly burned, toxic green lines crisscrossed over his charred skin. Emily rushed forward and placed her hands directly over the searing poison on Moonshadow's flanks.

A shudder went through her body as she felt the great wolf's pain. She could see the green aura of darkness emanating from the wolf, reaching for her like a gruesome specter. Then his heartbeat locked rhythm with hers, and Emily pulled the sickness from the wolf's body. She wrestled with the Black Fire, forcing its green glow away from the pack leader's shining silver magic. Ever so slowly, the green lines began to disappear and the flesh started to heal.

Emily whirled, covering as many wolves in healing light as fast as she could. She moved like a dancer, reaching the mistwolves with the power of her healing and restoring their true magic.

Then Zach, Emily, and Ozzie ran to the next crystal. Dragon stone raised, rainbow jewel ready, fierce ferret face steady.

"Ready?" Zach asked.

Emily nodded. "Go!"

∞

Something opened and something closed in Adriane's mind at the same time. She felt the mistwolves—they were free! She searched frantically through the voices in her head. But she couldn't find Storm's. She wanted to scream but was suddenly knocked to the ground as the throne room shuddered. Chunks of rock fell from the high ceiling, smashing to the polished floor.

The sorceress was on her feet moving toward the seeing pool.

Adriane braced herself against the shaking wall. Lyra paced back and forth snarling. The cat was okay, as far as Adriane could tell.

With a stir from her finger, the Dark Sorceress conjured an image in the pool—and her eyes went wide with rage.

One of the crystals had exploded, leaving a cloud of magic hanging over the lair. The mistwolves had been freed!

She whirled around to the star map, watching the oncoming wave. It was unbelievable—more magic than she'd even dreamed possible.

Then she turned to Adriane. "Your friends are destroying the crystals, releasing Black Fire. They would trade the lives of the mistwolves for the destruction of Aldenmor!"

"Either way, you won't control the magic," Adriane said cooly.

"Such a waste." The witch raised her arm, magic spinning from her long fingers. "The mistwolves cannot stand against my armies."

"Think again, loser," Adriane spat.

The sorceress's eyebrow raised in suspicion. She suddenly snapped her head as if hearing incredibly bad news and stared more closely into the pool. Her body was shimmering in anger, magic fire radiating around her.

Adriane steeled herself and faced the evil witch calmly. "What's the matter? Your monsters having a little *dragon* trouble?"

With a screech, the sorceress hurled magic at Adriane. Lyra knocked the warrior to the side as it hit the wall, ricocheting around the room. Adriane flung her arms and shot golden fire. The sorceress held up her hands, but Adriane pushed harder.

The witch's feral eyes opened wide. She was being pushed back by Adriane's power! What had happened? Adriane howled as the mistwolf pack sent their magic surging into her jewel. But it was not enough. They were at a stalemate and they both knew the sorceress was more experienced.

Suddenly, bright white light spilled into the chamber—a portal opened right in the middle of the throne room! Something horrible bellowed. The manticore stepped through.

Adriane gasped. It was more hideous than she remembered. Hunched over, the demon creature was enormous. Its huge apelike arms, rippling with muscle, hung down to the floor. Legs the size of tree trunks lumbered forward as it scraped its razor-sharp claws along the stone. Fire-red demon eyes scanned the room.

The beast's foul stench made Adriane cringe.

The sorceress laughed. "It seems my dark creature has eluded your dragon."

Adriane slowly backed away. There was no chance of beating this thing, she was just too exhausted. She stared at the monster and—did that thing just *wink* at her?

Adriane couldn't believe it. She looked to Lyra. The cat seemed to be—*smiling?*

The witch approached the manticore as the portal glowed behind her. "Take them!" she ordered.

"Oookee dookee."

What was that?

Something fluttered. Adriane looked closer.

Fiona, the red dragonfly, was sitting on the Dark Sorceress's head! The little d-fly peered into her face. "Peeyew!"

"Ahhhhhh!" the sorceress screamed, waving the creature away.

"Ahhhhh!" The little red dragonfly freaked and popped out.

Pop! Pop! Pop! Pop!

"Oooo, DeeDee!" Fred landed on Adriane's shoulder, nuzzling into her neck.

"What trickery is this?" the witch screamed at the manticore. "Kill them all!"

The creature's eyes flashed. It opened its razor-toothed mouth—and spoke. "I don't think so."

It wasn't the voice of a monster. It was—*Kara's* voice.

Adriane could feel the strong magic of her friend inside the thing. There was no doubt the creature was Kara.

The Dark Sorceress stared in shock. "How . . ."

But Adriane was already in front of her, wolf stone raised.

"Would you like to do the honors?" The manti-Kara held its twisted claws out to the portal.

Adriane stepped forward, her jewel blazing.

Shock registered across the witch's face.

Adriane looked at her jewel and lowered her arm.

"What I think she needs . . ." the warrior began, "is a little human touch."

With that, she connected—with a right cross! The sorceress flew backward, straight into the portal.

The dragonflies gleefully whizzed around the portal, spinning and twirling.

The manticore transformed, its huge body melting away to reveal a slim blond-haired girl in its place.

"You!" the witch stammered.

Lyra howled.

Kara waved at the Dark Sorceress. "Buh bye now."

For a moment, the sorceress's eyes remained visible, radiating hatred.

The dragonflies squeaked and chirped as the portal got smaller and smaller, until with a twinkle, it vanished—taking the sorceress with it.

Kara stood wiping her hands. "Pretty smelly, huh? What?"

Adriane looked at her in shock. "That was amazing! How did you do that?"

Kara smiled and waggled a sparkling jewel in her friend's face. "I got a jewel. I got a jewel."

Adriane raised an eyebrow. But before Kara could gloat some more, Emily's voice rang out in their minds, *"Adriane, come quickly!"*

19

K ARA, ADRIANE, AND Lyra entered the crystal chamber. It was in complete chaos.

Mistwolves were everywhere, snarling and growling; crystal shards littered the floor, sparking and crackling. The ceiling had been blown open, revealing thick clouds of green. Black Fire fallout engulfed them in a glittering, pulsing glow.

The mistwolves howled as Adriane ran into the fray, frantically searching for Storm.

"Kara!" Ozzie called. "Over here!"

Kara and Lyra found an exhausted Emily, still working to heal the wolves.

"Kara, are you all right?" Emily ran her hand over a brown-and-grey wolf and sent it on its way.

"I'm fine."

"What happened?" Emily asked.

"Never mind about me. How are you doing?" Kara wanted to know.

"The mistwolves are well enough to leave." Emily swept back sweat-streaked hair from her face.

"What's stopping them?" Kara asked

"They *refuse* to leave!" Zach ran to them, giving Kara a quick nod, then looked to the ceiling. "They're keeping the Black Fire from spreading."

The roiling fire pulsed and glowed around them. The cloud continued to darken, becoming almost black.

"I don't know what else to do!" Tears spilled down Emily's face. "I can't keep healing them!"

"Emily!" Kara held her friend's hands, looking deep into her eyes. "Remember when I asked you how far this thing would go?"

Emily nodded, sniffling.

"And why were we chosen?"

"Yes," Emily answered.

"We *weren't* chosen," Kara said. "We were the ones who chose!"

Emily looked at her friend. She was right. Emily had chosen to become a healer. Adriane had chosen to follow Storm on the warrior's path. And Kara had chosen to join them.

"Now we have to follow our path wherever it leads. With the help of our friends!" Kara turned to include everyone in the room. "And we choose now to finish this!"

"She's right!" Ozzie joined in. "The magic is sick and needs to be healed, just like all of you and the other creatures of Aldenmor."

"Gather around us!" Kara shouted. "Feed your magic to Emily. We will heal the magic!"

Suddenly, Emily, Kara, and Adriane, Ozzie, and Lyra were surrounded by a hundred mistwolves.

Emily rolled up her sleeves and concentrated. The rainbow jewel began to pulse with blue-green light. But the light was duller than usual, dimmed by the ominous black cloud.

"I need everyone's help," Emily told them.

Silence filled the room. The mistwolves shone with magic, sending their strength back into Emily's stone.

Ozzie's whiskers twitched as he hugged Emily tight. The rainbow jewel brightened, then pulsed.

Lightning flashed across the chamber. The walls shuddered as one collapsed in a cloud of dust and debris.

"*Stay together!*" Moonshadow ordered.

Kara turned to Adriane. "Are you ready?"

Adriane stood next to Kara and held out her hand.

Kara grasped it. "Ready, Emily?"

Emily nodded, placing her hand over those of her friends.

The healer raised her rainbow jewel, sending waves

of blue up and around her arms. Adriane raised her wolf stone, wrapping golden fire around Emily's blue magic.

Then Kara held up her unicorn jewel. It blazed like a diamond star.

Everyone watched in amazement as ribbons of blue and gold raced around Kara, covering her in magic. Fueled by the jewel of the unicorns, the magic built to a fiery crescendo.

"Let's do it!" she yelled, and let the magic go.

Magic fire burst from the three gems, streaming like rockets into the cloud above.

The cloud rippled into a whirlpool of power.

With all of their hearts, the three mages focused on healing the twisted magic.

"Emily, go!" Ozzie shouted.

Supercharged by her friends and Kara's new jewel, Emily had no fear, no hesitation. The light of her magic could pierce through any darkness, even the Black Fire. With a final breath, Emily drove her shield into the heart of the darkness and washed it away.

Suddenly, the clouds exploded upward and streaming rays of multicolored lights lit the sky.

The chamber rocked as another wall collapsed.

"Let's get out of here!" Ozzie yelled.

The mistwolves bolted, running from the chamber in a wave. Emily grabbed Ozzie, hoisting him into her arms as Kara and Lyra herded the final wolves out.

Dust flew and the rumbling grew louder.

"Adriane!" Kara screamed, grabbing the warrior and pulling her out of the chamber.

"Storm!" Adriane called out. But there was no reply. Only silence echoed from the emptiness in her heart.

"We have to go *now!*" Kara dragged Adriane into the hall.

With a thunderous boom, the chamber behind them collapsed in a pile of rubble.

The girls burst through the front doors and into the bright light of the Shadowlands.

The mistwolves fanned out to make sure no guards or monsters stood in their way. Nothing did. Word had spread fast. The reign of the Dark Sorceress was over.

"Zach!" Drake swooped down from the sky, stirring up eddies of dust as he landed. Zach ran to his friend, hugging the dragon tight.

The group made its way to the top of the dunes and looked to the skies.

It was incredible! Bands of light formed and drifted overhead, brightening into giant curtains rippling with reds, blues, oranges, and purples. Glittering colors swirled like pinwheels as magic rained from the sky.

The magic drifted through the air, over the Shadowlands, bathing everything in a fine, shimmering mist. The healing of Aldenmor had begun.

As the group watched, the land began to transform. Dry, blackened earth drank in the magic and sprouted tender grasses and wildflowers. Charred tree and shrub branches burst with lush leaves.

Emily felt giddy, hugging Ozzie tightly, laughing and crying at the same time. She let the rain wash over her, never wanting this feeling to end.

Kara sat next to Lyra, hugging her friend close. She took a deep breath, inhaling fragrant spring blossoms. In her hands, the unicorn jewel felt warm.

Zach stood next to Drake, the big dragon refusing to let the boy leave his side.

The mistwolves surrounded them, howling in song, reveling in the healing of their planet. But then the wolf-song grew somber, filled with sadness and loss.

On the windswept hillside, Adriane stood alone watching the magical light show.

Kara, Emily, Lyra, and Ozzie joined the warrior.

Tears welled in Emily's blue eyes. "There was nothing you could have done."

"I know," Adriane said.

"Storm saved us all." Moonshadow slowly approached Adriane, Zach at his side.

Kara and Emily put their arms around Adriane as the warrior leaned into them.

"No tears." Adriane wiped at her eyes. "She wouldn't want that."

"One mistwolf held a hundred of us," Moonshadow said. *"Do you know how she did that?"*

Adriane looked at the large black wolf.

"Because she was thinking of you. Her love for you gave her the strength."

"Thank you," Adriane smiled.

"We weep for your loss, warrior."

The group was startled by the new voices they heard.

"You have guided magic back to Aldenmor and the Fairy Glen." The voices of the Fairimentals echoed in their heads. *"And you have changed the future forever."*

20

"*W arrior.*"

Adriane stood in the meadow under the shade of the great tree, Okawa. Its branches glistened with greens as if it, too, rejoiced in the coming rains. But the bright rippling colors were in stark contrast to the rain that fell in Adriane's heart. Around her a hundred mistwolves, the entire pack, had gathered.

Moonshadow, Silver Eyes, and Zach approached her.

"*Will you lead us in the wolf song?*" Moonshadow asked. "*We will wish Stormbringer well on her journey to the spirit pack.*"

Adriane was honored to lead the sacred ritual, reserved for members of the pack only. She threw her head back and sang the wolf song from deep in her soul as it had been taught to her by her lost friend. The pack joined, sending their voices echoing across the Fairy Glen.

Slowly, the mistwolves walked away. Adriane, Zach, Moonshadow, and Silver Eyes watched soft grasses and rainbow flowers wave under the light breeze.

"I can't say good-bye," Adriane whispered.

"You don't have to," Zach said gently.

"*She is not lost to us, but a part of the spirit pack,*" Moonshadow said.

"*If you listen, they speak to us still from within.*" Silver Eyes brushed Adriane's side.

Adriane ran her hand over the pack mother's soft fur.

"*Hold on tight to every memory,*" Silver Eyes said. "*It is what makes your heart strong.*"

Adriane closed her eyes and let the memories come— memories of her and Storm. The first time she realized they could communicate. The two of them wrestling across the hills of Ravenswood. Storm helping her understand the magic, and friendship. And their journey—together and separately—to Aldenmor.

"When does it stop hurting?" Adriane struggled to stay strong.

"Not for a long time," Zach said. "But you go on and you *hold* on! Think about what Storm would want for you."

"I don't know if I can," Adriane said truthfully. Her

heart lay in pieces, locked away in a place she could not reach.

"*Wolf daughter,*" Silver Eyes said. "*You must not close your heart to those who love you.*"

From the corner of her eye Adriane caught movement. Silver Eyes was nuzzling a fuzzy mistwolf pup forward. "*It is time for the student to become the teacher,*" the pack mother said.

Dreamer shifted shyly on his white paws. The wolf pup lifted his head to the warrior mage.

Adriane knelt and gazed into the pup's deep green eyes. "I guess we're both alone now," she whispered.

Dreamer understood. He moved into Adriane's arms. Feelings flashed—anger, fear, sadness, and loss—but underneath, tenderness and beauty, the promise of hope, and a conviction to fight for love, the heart of a warrior.

Holding Dreamer in her arms, Adriane cried.

"*I'll always be with you.*"

Dreamer's wolf eyes filled with love. And the bond was forged like iron between the lone wolf and the lone warrior—forever.

∞

The Fairy Glen was packed.

Pegasi, wommels, brimbees, jeeran, brimbees, all the magical animals from Ravenswood had returned to a place they never thought they'd see again. The waters of the fairy lake sparkled and glistened, reflecting the bright colors of the sky and the shimmering white of the portal that hung open near the shore. The wondrous Fairy Glen, seen by so few, was renewed. The heart of Aldenmor beat strong once again.

Ozzie stood chattering with a group of wide-eyed elves, astonished to be at such an extraordinary place. Emily, Kara, and Lyra waited patiently as Adriane approached with Zach, Moonshadow, and Silver Eyes. Emily smiled as she noticed Dreamer walking protectively at the dark-haired girl's side.

No words were spoken. Just a warm embrace by each told Adriane how much she was loved, how much she was needed.

"The prophecy has come to pass." The soft windy voice belonged to Ambia, an Air Fairimental. A thicket of twigs, brush, and leaves tumbled together as Gwigg, an Earth Fairimental, appeared. The beautiful Watermental, Marina, swirled up from the blue-green lake, glittering in the sun.

The entire glade hushed at the presence of such magical creatures.

"Three mages have come to our aid and healed Aldenmor," Gwigg said. "One has followed her heart, and found the strength of a warrior." Gwigg rumbled by Adriane.

"One has seen in darkness and found the light of healing." Marina sent gentle waves rippling through the lake.

The Air Fairimental flitted over to Kara. "And one has changed completely and found—"

"A jewel!" Kara held up her unicorn jewel.

"—restraint!" Ambia twinkled.

"Oh, that too," Kara said, smiling.

"You changed from the prettiest to the ugliest," Lyra teased.

"Yeah, but I'm back. And I'm still a princess!" Kara giggled, then glanced at Emily and Adriane. "Long story."

The portal on the shores of the lake shone brightly. Glimmering curtains swirled open to reveal a sprawling web of curved and looping lines.

The crowd stared in wonder at the magic web.

The Fairimentals gathered at the portal. "It has been a long time since magic has flowed across the strands of the web."

"Did I release Avalon's magic?" Kara asked.

"We do not know," Gwigg rustled.

"But the prophecy . . . didn't we find Avalon?" Emily asked.

"The prophecy can only guide us," the Earth Fairimental explained. "It can mean different things. You make it your own as you walk your path."

"I was on this island," Kara insisted. "There were the most beautiful fairy wraiths there."

"There are wraiths and sylphs who guard the most special of magical places." Ambia fluttered on a cool breeze.

"What the blazing star found was the Gates of Avalon," Gwigg said.

The mages glanced at one another.

"The wraiths said we need a key," Kara said.

"That is correct," Gwigg replied.

"A key? What's in Avalon?" Emily asked.

Ambia shook her head sadly. "Avalon has been lost to us for a very long time."

Moonshadow stepped forward. *"In my spirit vision, I saw the crystal city, broken and covered in webs. It was a dark place."*

Gwigg trembled, twigs and leaves falling to the ground. "We fear for Avalon."

"I saw a different Avalon." Kara stepped forward. "It was beautiful, an incredible city sparkling with lights."

The animals gasped.

"It means the future is uncertain, in motion, constantly changing." Ambia twinkled brightly. "Still, the rain falls, covering Aldenmor with glorious magic. It is full of possibilities and also fraught with dangers."

"The Dark Sorceress has been exiled to the Otherworlds," Gwigg told the mages. "But even now, dark creatures are gathering to hunt the magic."

The voices of the Fairimentals echoed across the Fairy Glade. "Ravenswood is more important than ever now. You must protect the magic that has been seeded there."

"So it begins, mages," Ambia said. "You have proven yourselves by healing Aldenmor."

Marina drifted to the shore's edge. "Now you must open the Gates of Avalon, this is your destiny."

"Right on, which one is it?" Kara studied the many portals dotting the web.

"The fairy maps have been destroyed," Ambia told the mages. "You are mages now, you will find another way."

The image in the portal changed. Phel waved to them from a field of rainbow flowers.

"The Fairy Realms are ready to support you," Gwigg rumbled.

The portal shimmered as blue-green oceans appeared. Fountains of water erupted as sea dragons with merfolk upon their backs arched into the air.

"We stand with you, mages!" Kee-Lyn called from the back of Meerka.

The picture shifted to show hundreds of elves atop rolling green hills of the Moorgroves. They raised their arms in cheers. "Go, Ozzie!"

"*Ozymandius*," Ambia called out.

Ozzie shuffled forward and kneeled before the wisp of wind.

"For your heroism and loyalty, you are hereby decreed a Knight of the Circle, a special protector of Avalon. Rise, Sir Ozymandius."

A twinkle of light suddenly glowed in the ferret's paws. When the light faded, Ozzie held a glittering golden stone. His eyes widened. "A ferret stone!" he shouted, showing his jewel to the astonished elves.

Everyone cheered at this amazing honor.

"The first mage from our village!"

Crusp and Tonin and the rest of Ozzie's relatives proudly puffed up their chests, patting their newly famous elf kin on the back.

"Thanks! But . . . can I change back to my real body?" Ozzie scratched his ear.

Ambia circled the ferret. "If you choose to stay here on Aldenmor, you may return to your elf body and honor us with your service."

"Yes!"

"But if you choose to return with the mages and join them on their quest, you must remain as you are."

"Oh." Ozzie looked to the elves and turned to Emily. Emily bit her lip.

Ozzie shuffled back and forth, fraught with indecision. "What should I do?" he asked, clearly torn.

"What you've always told us, Ozzie," Emily smiled. "You have to follow your heart."

Ozzie's brow crinkled as he clutched his new jewel and walked to the elf clan.

The animals of Ravenswood crowded around Kara, admiring her unicorn jewel.

"It is magnificent," Balthazar said.

"It sure is!" Then Kara smiled humbly. "But you guys are the ones who deserve this, not me."

"Nonsense," Rasha said. "Your magic comes from within, the jewel is just a reflection of your true beauty."

"Thank you." Kara hugged the animals that had become so close to her over the past months.

"Kara." Gwigg tumbled to a halt near her feet. "The blazing star faces the hardest lessons of all in the days ahead."

"Right, but what about the Skultum's magic?" Kara queried. "You know, that fairy stuff about absorbing its powers."

"It is hard to say if you will keep it. You are not skilled enough to sustain that level of power," Gwigg responded.

"I see." Kara scrunched her nose. The jewel warmed and flashed—and her hair turned bright purple!

"Ooo!" The animals admired her choice of color.

Quickly, before anyone else could notice, she turned her hair back to blonde.

"The magic runs deep inside you now," Gwigg warned. "It is a gift. To use your powers impulsively only makes you more and more dependent on them. You must be careful lest you fall under its darker pull."

"What do I do?" Kara asked, suddenly worried.

"Stand strong with your friends," Ambia advised, leading Kara to the bright light.

Kara walked to the portal next to Adriane and Emily. The three girls clasped hands.

Ozzie and the elves were in deep conversation, then did a lot of hugging and more hugging. Emily watched as the ferret walked away from the elves to stand next to her.

"I'm going to miss you, Ozzie," Emily sniffled.

"Why, where are you going?" Ozzie looked confused, then smiled. "'Cause wherever it is, I'm going, too."

Kara, Lyra, Emily, Ozzie, Adriane, and Dreamer stood before the portal that would take them home. As the rainbow of lights twinkled in the skies over the Fairy Glen, they knew one thing for sure. Their friendship would see them through any new challenges and adventures they would face in the struggles ahead. They had saved Aldenmor. But the mages had learned that the power to triumph over evil was ultimately not in the magic itself, but something more powerful: the magic of the ties that bound humans and animals, nature, and all living things—that is the spirit of Avalon.

Bestiary &
Creature Guide

Firemental

Neutral

$\mathcal{T}$he most powerful and dangerous of the Fairimentals, the Firemental only appears in the most dire and desperate situations. Made completely of elemental fire, it is unstable, unpredictable, and extremely rare.

GOBLIN

NEUTRAL

*G*oblins are a diverse race of beings that occupy a wide range of areas on the magic web. Some have been employed as mercenaries for the Dark Sorceress, trained in the dark arts of magic. Other goblins are more peaceful, occupying the Goblin Kingdom in the Fairy Realms.

Sea Dragon
Good

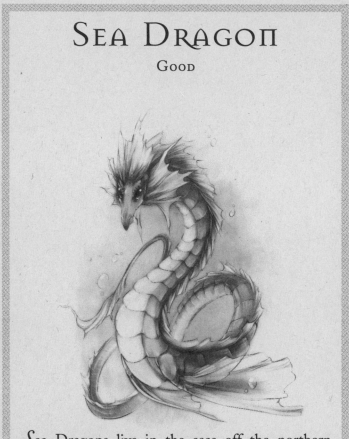

$\int$ea Dragons live in the seas off the northern coasts of Aldenmor. Revered and loved for generations by merfolk as trusted allies and bonded friends, sea dragons are loving and very loyal.

Night Stallion

Evil

*N*ight stallions are fearsome mounts trained to serve evil minions of dark magic. They are powerful fire breathing horselike beasts. Night stallions make a fearsome cavalry for the Dark Sorceress's army

RACHEL ROBERTS
ON THE SPIRIT
OF AVALON

*T*HE SPIRIT OF Avalon is alive in horses running across the plains, dolphins playing in the ocean, and the hummingbirds buzzing across my backyard. We share our world with so many diverse animals, magnificent creatures big and small. It's their home too. Keeping wild places wild allows us to experience the magic each creature has to share. We can keep the spirit alive in our own way. The mages protect the animals of Aldenmor. You can speak for the endangered creatures of Earth and their habitats. Every animal deserves a home where wild places are safe and wild things run free.